Anal Adventures

25 Hot Erotica Stories of Extreme Anal Sex

By: Victoria Gray

Forward

Hello and thank you for checking out my book. I wrote these erotic adventures to entertain others and I've them some great stories about anal sex. I hope you enjoy them!

Table of Contents

Mandy's First Experience

Mandy sighed, feeling like everything was going to the toilet. After a big breakup, her job driving her bad, and stress, the last thing she wanted to do was to deal with anyone. But, her best friend Jasmine insisted upon seeing a guy, so that's what she did, even though this normally wasn't her scene at all.

That's why Mandy was here, in the club with a bunch of random people. But none of them were catching her attention. That is, until a muscular man with sandy blonde hair and blue eyes caught her eye. She looked at him, and the look sealed the deal. He marched over to her, smiling at her with a devilish grin.

"You alone?"

"Yeah. Recently broke up with my shitty ex. Could use a pick-me-up," she admitted.

"Want me to show you something different, but fun?" he inquired.

Mandy looked at him, slightly unsure as to what that meant. But, this was her first time experiencing freedom in forever, so she immediately said yes.

The man, who she learned shortly after was named Randy, took her hand, practically gliding her to the hotel across the street from the club. Soon, his lips were on her own, and Mandy immediately responded.

He was a good kisser, and the fact that he used tongue turned her on even more. She rutted her hips against his cock, feeling the bulging muscle against there. He smiled, pulled away and touching her hips.

"Eager are we?"

"Yes," she replied.

"There is one thing I'd like to ask of you, and that is...I want to try putting it in your ass," he said.

Put it in her ass? That seemed so bizarre.

"Are you sure? I've never done that before."

"I wouldn't mind trying it. If it's too much, I won't continue. But I'lll make sure you're prepared," he said.

Mandy was hesitant, but she soon agreed, and Randy pushed her onto the bed, kissing her passionately. He soon tore off her clothes, leaving her naked and flush. His hands moved up, touching the bud of the nipple, and she soon gasped, feeling her body jerk in response. He teased the edge of her bud, letting his hands dance over the area. His lips moved to the other bud, teasing it with his lips, and Mandy immediately groaned.

He moved down her body towards the folds of her pussy, spreading her apart and using his hands to both penetrate her and tease her clit. He was like a professional with this, surprising Mandy as he started to push his fingers into there, teasing her pussy with every single touch. He inserted one finger, and then the second, all while circling her clit with his thumb.

The sensations were almost too much. Not even her ex was this good. She tensed up, moaning out loud as she came hard, feeling her body squeeze his fingers and then relax.

"You good?" he asked.

"Yes."

"You want to try it still?" Randy inquired.

Mandy nodded, trusting this guy.

"You prepared me better than my ex ever did, so I'lll try it," she said.

He smiled, moving his index finger downwards, teasing her pucker. He reached towards his pocket, grabbing the lube and putting it on. With deft hands, he inserted the first finger, causing her to suddenly gasp at the intrusion.

It was a stretch, that's for sure, but he soon pushed the digit in deeper, causing her to gasp at the sensation of it. It felt so full, so nice, and while he inserted the fingers, he teased her clit with small touches. He was a natural at this, and as Mandy started to feel him put a third in, she realized he was met with little resistance.

She never thought doing it in the butt would feel so fucking good.

He started to dance his fingers in and out, penetrating her softly, and as she felt this, she began to tense up, feeling her body immediately respond in a positive manner to this. After the third finger was inside completely, she spoke.

"I want your cock," she said.

"Good to know. Want it missionary?" he asked.

"Y-yes," Mandy said.

She figured for her first time it would be good. He spread her apart, pulling his pants off to reveal his large, seven-inch cock. It was throbbing, and for a moment, Mandy wondered if she could get that inside her. But then, he gently pushed in, and soon it was all the way in.

It was a bit of a discomforting tightness, but then she grew used to it, moaning in pleasure at the sensations bestowed to her. He began to thrust, pushing in and out of her hole, and each one hit her in a different spot than being fucked in the pussy ever did. He pulled her hips up, pushing deep into her, and with deep, penetrative thrusts, she screamed.

His hand moved up to her clit, teasing her there, and soon he dipped two fingers into her pussy, fucking both of her holes. Mandy never felt so fucking full, and as she felt him push in deeper and deeper, she could feel the onset of her orgasm come over her.

When it did, she squeezed against him, causing him to groan and release inside her. She didn't expect him to do that, but it felt so amazing that she didn't want him to stop. When it was over, he pulled back, looking at her with a smile on his face.

"You enjoy that?"

"Yeah. I wouldn't mind doing that again," Mandy admitted.

He reached up, kissing her softly on the lips.

"Well if you ever need some butt fun, I'm always ready for that," he said.

Mandy nodded, taking that into consideration. It was a simple one-night stand, but it woke up something within Mandy that changed her forever.

She was a butt slut now, and she wanted nothing more than to be fucked in the ass again, especially be a thick, hard cock.

Spicing It Up

Angela wanted to try this. She heard from her friend Mia that anal is amazing, and with the right cock, she knew she was in for a treat.

That's why, when she felt the throes of pleasure from the stimulation her husband Paul provided to her, Angela knew for a fact that this was it. She felt enraptured in pleasure, and when Paul pulled back from her aching cunt, which was dripping in both saliva and her own juices, he pushed his hands to his mouth, wiping the contents and smiling.

"Was that good babe?"

"Yeah. Fucking amazing," Angela admitted with a blush.

He looked at her, and as he pointed to the toys, Angela nodded. She wanted to try this with Paul. He wasn't huge, but he also wasn't tiny, so he would fit pretty tightly within her. She did try masturbating once with her ass along with her vibrator, and it gave her some of the best orgasms of her life.

She felt his hands touch her pucker, just massaging the area there. Angela tensed, realizing how different, but also how nice this felt. He then slipped his hand back, grasping the lube and putting it onto his hands. Angela looked at Paul with an anticipatory glance, knowing full well that her husband wouldn't hurt her.

With ginger hands, he pushed the first digit in. Angela tensed, feeling the foreign sensation within her. She loved it, but at also at the same time didn't know what to think of it. He pushed his hands into her, fingering her ass with his digits, and she soon relaxed, moaning to the touch. Her body clenched up, and while he continued to tease her, his tongue moved between her legs, licking at her clit.

She relaxed, moaning at the sensations she was given. He soon added in a second digit, teasing the area there, and it was then when she began moaning in his ear, feeling everything start to change within, her whole body reacting to his touches in a manner that she wasn't used to. As he continued to finger her, moving the digits around, he touched the area against her body that sent jolts through her body. Angela cried out, and as she did so, Paul let his tongue move towards her clit, touching and teasing her.

"Fuck, fuck fuck!" she cried out, feeling the desperation and the need for more start to overtake her. She loved everything about this, and then, when she felt the aftereffects of her orgasm start to diminish, she looked at Paul, who smiled at her.

"You good?"

"Yeah. Better than good," she admitted.

He smiled, pushing her legs further apart. He pushed a third digit in, and Angela immediately felt the tightness against the ring of muscle. She felt her entire body grow tense, especially due to how stuffed up she was. He thrust his hands in and out of her, deeper and deeper, and Angela was struggling to keep her consciousness there. She could feel another orgasm come about, and when it all hit her, she tensed up, crying out loud and in pleasure as she came hard against his hands, shivering in delight.

He pulled back, smiling as he looked at her.

"Do you want to be on top?" he asked.

"Sure," she replied.

Angela felt nervous when it came to this, and soon, she moved her body so that her ass was right over his lubed cock. When she moved down on it, she immediately felt the ongoing tightness that came along with it, screaming out loud and in pleasure at the sensations of this. She then started to ride his cock, tensing up and moaning out loud at the sensations that were riding through her body. After a few more thrusts, she then felt him grasp her hips, pushing in and out of her hard.

Angela couldn't believe the sensations she was feeling through her body. It was strange, mostly because she never thought that she'd get a chance to experience pleasure in this way, but as he penetrated her, filling her up and also teasing her pussy with his fingers, Angela knew that the desperation for more touch, for more from her husband, the man that she loved, drove her mad.

"God I'm close," he said.

She looked at Paul, who had a look of desperation in his eyes. He seemed just as happy to have this happen as she did, his whole body reacting to her actions. After a few more thrusts, she then felt him tense against her, and she then noticed his hands as they moved up, penetrating her hard as he soon pushed his cock as deep into her as possible. With a groan, he came inside, and that's when Angela felt it.

The combination of him cumming inside and her own personal pleasure was too much, and she then cried out, tensing up as she soon released as well, feeling her orgasm completely overtake her. She moved off his cock, the cum trickling out of her ass as a result of their efforts, and when she looked at it, she smiled.

"That was fun," she admitted.

"Sure was. I didn't hurt you or anything, right?" Paul asked, worry that he might've hurt his wife obvious in his eyes.

"No, you're totally fine. In fact, I think I found my new favorite thing to do in the bedroom," Angela said with a purr. She looked at Paul, who blushed as well, and soon she gave him a deep kiss that expressed her adoration.

"Good. I'm glad I didn't hurt you. I love you babe," he said.

"I love you too."

Angela curled up to Paul, ignoring the cum that was in her ass for now. She was happy, and she knew that this adventure was one that she would love to go on again and again, and she knew that she would enjoy it no matter what would come about in the future.

The Anal Surprise

Hannah trusted her boyfriend when he said he wanted to try something new with her, but she would be in control.

However, she didn't expect it to be anal. But, when his hands moved towards her thighs, touching them, she looked down at Rob, who smiled at her.

"Are you okay babe?" he asked.

"Yeah. I'm just nervous. I've never done this before," she said.

"Well, if you're worried, or if you're in pain period, we can always stop. I promise that I'lll never hurt you," he admitted.

Hannah looked at Rob, noticing how honest he was, and she soon nodded.

"Okay. I trust you on this. But, how are you going to...prepare me?" she asked.

"I bought a couple of toys for this," he said.

Hannah watched as he brought forth a bottle of lube, along with a butt plug that looked small enough. She blushed at the contents, but then, Rob started to spread her folds open, diving his tongue into her sweet pussy. He licked in all the right places, and soon, Hannah's hands moved straight to his hair, teasing it slightly, and as he did this, she began to gasp.

"Fuck, this is just too good!" she cried out.

"You know I want to make you feel good baby," he said to her.

She blushed, but then she started to lose herself in the pleasures of the moment. She began to feel his tongue circle her clit, teasing it there as he began to push the toy inside. She expected it to hurt, expected it to be painful for her, and she expected it to be too much and she would refuse, but it went in so perfectly that she enjoyed the unfamiliar tightness that went along with it.

Rob took his time, letting the plug sit all the way in as he went to town, dining on her ripe pussy, and Hannah started to tense up, gripping the sheets as she felt the onset of her orgasm start to come about. She then lifted her hips up, moaning as she felt her body release. Rob accepted the juices, letting his mouth take care of cleaning her up before he pulled back.

"Are you good?"

"Yeah. I am. I want to try more," she said.

Rob grabbed a bigger butt plug, and soon, he pulled out the smaller one, causing a gasp to emit from her mouth. He then pushed the larger one into there, and Hannah felt the stretch this time, but I wasn't anything too bad.

"You good?"

"Yeah babe. I like the feeling," she said.

Rob started to play with the butt plug, pushing it in and out, and that's when Hannah felt a strange trickle of pleasure. She didn't expect it to feel so good, but then as he started to penetrate her deeper, she soon began to feel the difference. She knew for a fact that this was indeed something she could get used to, and then, just a few mere minutes later, Rob then began to move a bigger butt plug into her.

She felt the stretch this time, her body initially at first shocked by all of this, but then later on, she felt the urge to accept this. She then started to moan, feeling the excitement from everything that was happening, and soon, Rob started to thrust the toy in and out. Hannah cried out, feeling a strange pleasure within her body as she soon came hard.

When Rob finished, he pulled the toy out, looking at Hannah's spent body.

"Want to try it with the real thing?" he offered.

Hannah knew that Rob was bigger than the toys, so it made her feel slightly apprehensive. But then, she nodded, gripping the bed as he spread her apart. He undid his pants, pulling his cock out and stroking it.

"Fuck, you look so good right here," he said.

"Thank you. I'm glad," she admitted.

Rob then spread her cheeks apart, easing into there. At first, Hannah cringed at the sudden feeling of tightness, unsure of whether or not she was fine with it. It was then when he pushed all the way in, causing her to tense up at the sensations of this, her body aching for more.

He pushed his cock all the way into her, immediately causing her to let out a moan of pleasure, her entire body losing control at the sudden fullness. She then watched rob spread her pussy open, pushing a small vibrator into there.

"For real?" she asked.

"Yes. I want you to feel good," he said.

Hannah was so happy that Rob cared about her pleasure, and soon, he started to push the toy all the way in, turning it on and watching as she screamed out, the feeling of both her holes being penetrated being the most amazing thing ever. He soon started to thrust hard, but Hannah didn't care, because her entire body was at the mercy of all of the stimulation that she managed to feel at this point. She knew for a fact that rob was too good, and she knew that he was ready to make her feel good. It was then that, after a couple more thrusts, she felt her entire body tense up, her pussy completely dripping in pleasure, and she soon came hard. She felt her whole body completely lose itself, and she noticed that Rob came shortly after, but she didn't even feel it because she was so wrapped up in the pleasure that she felt.

Rob then pulled out, and Hannah simply laid there, completely spent from the feeling that she experienced. This was her first time experiencing this type of sex, and she knew that it woke something up within her.

The need to do it more and more.

She looked at Rob, smiling weakly, and it was then when she realized that Rob enjoyed it too, and they probably would end up doing this again sometime in the future.

The Neighbor's Love for Butt

When Nikki started messing around with her neighbor Caleb, she realized that the sex was out of this world. He knew how to make Nikki cum buckets, and it was something that not even her ex Toby could do. She didn't even need to use a toy or anything, because Caleb would touch her in all the right places, and she would become a melted puddle of pleasure.

But then, as she looked at Caleb this time, with the toy in his hands, she immediately grew nervous.

"You want to put that...in my butt?" she asked.

"Yeah. I wanted to try it for a while, but I didn't want to just spring this on you, because I didn't want to oops it into the back door, you know," he said with a smirk.

Nikki hesithated. She heard that this would hurt. But she looked at Caleb, and she knew that he was gentle enough with her that she could trust him.

"O-okay, but is it cool if I get into position? And I want you to take it slow," she said.

"That's fine dear. Trust me, I know that it's not something you're used to, but I promise that I'lll make sure that you're comfortable," he said.

Nikki trusted him, and that's something she couldn't always say about others. She got on the bed with her ass up, and as she felt

Caleb spread her legs, teasing the very edge of her thighs, she felt her body become a melted puddle of pleasure. She moaned, experiencing the pleasure that came forth with this, and soon, he started to spread her apart, pressing a small bullet vibrator right into her pussy lips. Nikki cried out, tensing up as she felt the vibrations start to swim through her body.

This felt too good. How could this feel so good?

She then felt his hands spread her ass cheeks apart, his hands teasing her pucker with small dancelike touches. She tensed up, letting her body immediately respond to his actions, and soon, he grasped a bottle of something. She imagined it was lube, and after he uncapped it and spread the contents onto his fingers and the toy, she immediately tensed up.

He gingerly pushed a finger into there, spreading her apart with the small touch. It was tight, but Nikki loved it, and she soon began to moan as the neighbor thrust his fingers in and out of her a little bit faster, making his motions almost a bit rough in a sense. She began to moan at the sensations that were given to her, the sudden tightness a bit of a shock to her, but then as he pushed the second finger into there, she soon began to moan even more, tensing up as she felt him push his fingers in a penetrative manner deep into her. She loved this, and soon, he began to move his fingers in and out, faster and faster, and it was then when she felt his hand tease the toy inside her pussy. She immediately felt her body tense up, feeling the excitement grow within, and when he pushed the toy up slightly, she cried out, feeling the throes of her orgasm as it took over her.

When she relaxed, she soon watched as he pushed back, and when Nikki stared at the neighbor, he smiled at her before he pulled back, smirking.

He took the toy out, causing Nikki to cry out, the pleasure and feeling of emptiness beginning to take over her. He then spread her cheeks apart, and then, the sound of the uncapping of lube was heard, and she soon looked over.

He stroked his cock, smiling at her as she blushed. Nikki was excited for this man to take her first time, her anal virginity, and when he pushed the dip against her hungry hole, she shivered.

"Fuck," she said to him.

"You like that babe?"

"Yeah. it's good," she replied, flushing red.

He then started to push himself into her, and the sudden tightness overwhelmed her, and soon, she started to cry out. It was then when he pulled her back so that she could control the speed of his cock going in, and then with small thrusts, Nikki got the rest of his aching dick into her ripe pussy. She shivered, feeling her body tense up with shock at the sensations that she felt. She then started to move slightly, pressing down against him, but then he bucked his hips up, suddenly moving towards her, and when he did, she screamed out.

"Fuck!"

"You okay?"

"Yes, do that again!"

Nikki felt the desperation grow within her, and she soon watched as he began to move his hips up and down against her, his body aching with need. He started to press up and down against her, pushing faster and faster against her, and she soon cried out as he slammed his cock against her body. She felt it all the way in her body, and when he pushed the entire length of his cock into her, and he pushed the toy that he had against her clit, she screamed out, suddenly feeling her body cum hard.

She felt his cock pull out, covering her ass with his cum. She shivered as she felt the spurts of cum against there, and when he finally finished up, he pulled away, smiling at her.

Nikki felt like she experienced a heavenly sensation, her body wanting more, but her mind completely exhausted. She fell down onto the bed, falling asleep shortly after. Caleb was soon right next to her, and when she cuddled up to his larger body, she felt happy and satisfied. She would love to try anal again, and she knew that Caleb enjoyed it just as much as she did as well. They'd both try to plan another experience such as this, and Nikki knew for sure he was as desperate as she was for more, so much more than she expected to feel.

The housewife's Love For Anal

Carrie loved anal, and when she saw the face of exertion that her younger neighbor had it made her shiver. He pushed his cock against the edge of her pucker, teasing her there, and when she felt the slight ache of the burn when he probed her like this, she groaned.

"Fuck," she said.

"You good?" Derrick asked. That was the name of the younger neighbor, and he was a total looker. With sandy blonde hair, blue eyes, and tall frame with bulging muscles, Carrie loved it whenever they had their romps together after she sent off her daughter Abby to school. Usually it involved just fucking and having a bit of fun, nothing serious because she didn't want to worry about that, but when Derrick offered to try anal the first time, she was initially hesitant, but then as he spread her apart, pushing his cock into her the first time, she knew that she made the right choice.

It was heavenly to feel his dick inside there, and while it was originally something that made Carrie shiver at first, and question whether or not she wanted this, but as she continued to feel the cock slowly sink in, filling her up completely, it made her want to enjoy more and more. It was then when he started to fuck her mercilessly into the sheets and while Carrie never thought that she'd love anal like this, she knew that with Derrick, she could enjoy this now.

And here she was, with the thick cock right near her entrance, slowly sinking in, and as he continued to more in with every single inch, she started to take a deep breath, relaxing her muscles as he pushed all the way into her.

She shivered as she began to feel him completely fill her up, and it was then when she started to feel everything tense up and then relax, she knew that this was the experience that she wanted, the one that she desired more than anything else.

He groaned as he filled Carrie up, and Carrie knew for a fact that he was enjoying this just as much as she was. He soon pushed all the way in, and when he pushed his cock deep into her, sheathing himself deeply against her ass, she felt everything penetrate deeply. After being asked by Derrick if she was cool, and the response of a resounding yes, he soon started to thrust into her, immediately pushing deep into her and fucking her relentlessly. She pushed her ass up, meeting his cock with the heavy thrusts, and when he pushed all the way in, she felt the familiar tightness, one that she knew and loved.

"Fuck yes! Give me more of your fucking cock!" Carrie cried out, her entire body losing control as she felt it go deeper and deeper. She could practically feel her insides being completely filled by his dick, and when she realized that she was already getting close, she relished in it.

But of course, Derrick wanted to give her some extra attention too. With deft hands, he moved towards her pussy, fingering her deep with his digits and rolling a thumb against there. Immediately, Carrie felt her entire body get kicked into overdrive. Despite having her daughter, Carrie was still extremely sensitive down there, and as she felt him start to penetrate her harder and harder, she felt her body begin to lose control, the only thing happening being the screams of pleasure that exuded from her mouth.

When she came hard, she felt like everything was a blur. She loved how her orgasms felt whenever she got fucked in the ass. They were deeper more penetrative, and they hit every single part of her being, her entire body losing control of it all, and everything becoming a blur.

After she relaxed, she felt him start to push deeper and deeper into her, and Carrie was mesmerized by the sthate of his body. He was desperate, with sheens of sweat on his face, and then, after a few more thrusts, he cried out, groaning in pleasure as he soon came deep within her, his cum hitting every inch of her being, and filling the walls of her tight, hot ass.

When he pulled out, he sat back, looking at Carrie with a happy smile.

"You good?”

"Yes dear. I'm definitely happy with the results this time around. You've definitely gotten better,” she said.

"That's because I have such a good teacher. I mean, you're so good, and you teach me how to really make you happy. I mean, you're the first woman I've truly been able to pleasure, and it makes me happy knowing this," he admitted.

When she heard this, she felt both happy, but also a little bit surprised by it all. She looked at him, and he soon spoke.

"I want to keep doing this with you. I mean, I know that you have the daughter, and yeah she's getting older, but I don't want to lose you Carrie. You're like, the best person I've met, and I like doing this,” he said.

Carrie smiled, pulling him close and stroking his cock, smirking at the look that he had on his face.

"Well, you don't have to worry about me leaving, because I have no plans to. Now come on, let's go for another round,” she told Derrick with a purr.

And it was then when the younger man followed the MILF's lead, letting her stroke his cock to hardness again. Carrie took control, as she loved to do, and when she was able to blow him again, and from there have him fuck her again in both her pussy and ass, she loved every moment of it. This was something that

23

she didn't regret doing, and she realized over time that it was something that she didn't regret at all in her life.

Forest Anal Adventures

For Gina, the one thing that she didn't expect her boyfriend Luke to do was push her up against a tree in the middle of a forest and make out with her. But they were alone, and public sex was totally a thing for her, but she didn't expect it out here, in the middle of the forest during the day.

But that didn't stop Gina from kissing, and as Luke kissed her back, grinding his cock against her, she got this idea. Gina had recently become fascinated with anal, even to the point of doing it with Luke a little bit. It was awkward, that's for sure, but they always managed to have a lot of fun with it, and Gina never complained.

They never did it out in public though, and when Gina pulled away, she looked at her boyfriend with a smoldering smile, desperation obvious on her face.

"I want you to fuck my ass till I can't move," she said to him.

Those words were enough to sir Luke on, for he pushed her against the tree, furiously making out with her for what seemed to be forever before his hands slipped to her pussy, teasing her through the confines of her pants. Gina moaned, feeling the heat start to grow, and the aching throb within her body.

He continued to tease for a minute until he pulled away, moving his hands to the waistband of her pants. With a swift motion, he slipped them off, pushing his face into her pussy, and his hands

25

towards her pucker. Gina didn't know when he managed to put on lube, but soon a probing finger was in there. She immediately reacted to the touch, moaning in pleasure as she felt him penetrate her ass as he continued to eat her out. Gina tried to stay quiet, but the little motions were more than enough for her, and in her mind, she felt like she was experiencing a little taste of heaven.

"Fuck, fuck!" she screamed out loud, trying to hold herself back. He continued to eat her out, teasing every inch of her folds and her body reacting to his own sweet touches. It was heavenly, and then, after a few more moments, she felt a second finger enter into her.

She wanted his cock. She immediately pulled back, slamming her body against the tree, ass out and ready for him.

"Please, just cut the crap will you? I want you to fuck my ass," she moaned, her hips wiggling to help punctuate the need for him.

Luke didn't need to be told twice. He soon spread her cheeks apart, grasping the very tiny bottle of lube he had on himself for moments like this, and he poured the contents straight onto his cock, groaning at the sudden feeling that this gave to him. He looked at Gina, who had a flushed face, her hips out, and her ass looking hungry for action. He immediately pushed the tip inside, sliding his hard member straight into her, causing her to immediately moan in response.

"Holy fuck!" she screamed out loud, immediately tensing up at the sudden feeling. But then, just as quick as it was to happen, she soon felt him press all the way in, filling her pussy up with the sweet tightness.

She immediately shuddered, feeling everything change within her. It felt so right, so perfect, and then, as he started to push in and out of her ass, the tightness overwhelming, she felt it hit all of the right angles. She loved anal, and the fact that she was here, pushed straight up against a tree, being fucked mercilessly by the man that she loved, immediately turned her on even more, and the only thing heard from her was a cacophony of moans.

She noticed Luke's hands right by her pussy, fingering her wet cunt and pushing two fingers into there while he slammed his cock straight into her. The sudden force of the push, and the tightness and fullness of her hole as he pushed all the way in, turned her on even more, and then, after a few brief moments, she felt him push in deeper and deeper, pistoning his cock in and out of her. She immediately moaned in pleasure, her entire body feeling the effects of it all, and then, when he pushed a finger inside of her pussy, curling it up to that bundle of nerves that she knew and loved, she screamed out loud, and it was then when everything changed.

With a shudder, she came hard, feeling the throes of her orgasm completely decimate her. When she finally finished, she felt Luke punctuate two more deep thrusts straight into her, and then, after the third, he groaned, immediately pushing himself all the way in and shuddering at the tightness that came along with her orgasm. She felt her entire body lose control, and that's when Gina realized that Luke indeed finished all the way inside her. He pulled back, putting his cock away as Gina pulled her pants up.

"Well that was a bit of fun," she said.

"Sure was. I think we definitely were a bit loud though," he said.

She heard the sound of footsteps nearby, and Gina knew immediately that someone did hear them. She smiled to herself, feeling both accomplished yet fearful at the realization of this. They both grasped one another's hands, each of them getting away from the scene of where they were.

It was an adventurous romp, and Gina would totally do it again. Next time though, they'd have to make sure that they didn't have anyone else nearby, and they'd have to pay attention to the sounds that were being made.

But, Gina and Luke smiled to one another, and despite the fact that there was a lot of cum in Gina's ass, she'd do this again, and she knew that Luke would certainly do the same thing.

Anal Art Inspiration

Carli struggled to paint the rest of her picture. She needed some inspiration, something that would help her keep on going, a reason for continuing on this pathway.

What she didn't expect, was for Darren to call her, saying that he would come over to the studio to help.

Darren was her current fling, almost to the point of boyfriend level. They were implicitly together, but they never announced it on social media or any shit, but when he came inside, they both hugged one another tightly, making out shortly after. Tongues began to move in perfect synchronization with one another, and then, as Carli pulled away, she looked at him with a huff.

"I need inspiration," she said.

"What kind?"

"I don't know, I just feel that all of my art is...boring. I feel like I need to spice this up. I've been painting erotically, but I want to try something new," she admitted.

Carli blushed as Darren looked her over, smirking in excitement. His hand moved up towards her ass, holding it there in his hands and cupping it. She gasped, feeling the sudden excitement and need for whatever was about to come next.

"I mean...I could show you something new," he said.

Carli was familiar with what he was talking about. Anal. She noticed that Darren was very into the idea of anal sex, but she never really was interested. That is until now. She did practice with a plug a couple of times before today, but something seemed different this time. She felt that their connection was stronger, and as she moved towards the touch, she smirked.

"I wouldn't mind that," she said.

"Good. I'lll make it worth your while then," he said.

He pushed her onto the art bench, and soon, his hands moved towards her pants, pulling them down and off her body. Carli gasped at the sudden feeling of this, realizing just what was going on. His hands moved skillfully, like an artist at the canvas, against her pussy, teasing her with small, needy touches. Immediately, Carli moaned, feeling her entire body move against Darren's hands. His hands were skillful, and as he tore her art smock off her body, he pressed his hands to an erect nipple, sucking on this slightly. Carli gasped, feeling everything change within her, and as she began to feel him move his tongue against there, she began to immediately tense up, moaning out loud at his motions. She then watched as he pulled back, smiling at her before he soon pushed his hands towards her ass.

"I brought something for this moment," he said.

It was lube. She could smell it, a strong strawberry flavor that was chill and perfect. He then pushed the first finger into there, letting his hands move towards her pussy, teasing her in both of her holes.

Carli gasped, immediately feeling everything change. This was so perfect, so nice, and as she felt him continue these actions, her body ached for more. Her pussy throbbed for more of his touch, and as he continued to do this, she knew for a fact that he was enjoying this just as much as she was.

"You good babe?" he asked.

"Yes. I want your cock though," she said.

"Good. How do you want it?" he asked.

She looked over near the bench that was by the canvas that she was working on.

"Over there. Take me from behind," she uttered.

Darren didn't need to be told twice. He soon raced over, pushing her against the bench, grasping her hips, and soon his cock sank into her. She groaned, suddenly shocked by the intrusion, but then her ass got used to it as he sank into her, gasping in pleasure at the sensations that he felt.

She immediately moaned as he filled her ass up with his cock. He thrust in deep, letting his hands play with her nipples from behind. The tweaking sensations, along with the feeling of his cock, drove her mad, and as she felt each of these sensations, she looked over at Darren, who was grinning at her with a dark glance.

"This feels...so good," she told him.

"Anything for you princess," he told her with a purr.

He soon fucked her harder and harder, thrusting in so deep that she felt like her entire body was being driven mad by all of this. He soon fucked her faster and faster, shoving a couple of fingers into her wet cunt, thrusting in deep. With each and every single penetrative action, Carli felt like she was losing her mind, and then after a few more thrusts he pushed all the way in, making her tense up, cry out loud, and then cum hard.

The sudden feeling of this drove her mad. She then tensed up, immediately gasping as she finished against him. His cock then pushed all the way in, and with one final groan, he came hard inside of her. The two of them finished up, and when it was all said and done, Darren pulled back. He turned to give her a kiss, and soon, he spoke.

"You good babe?" he asked.

"Yeah. I'm definitely happy with this," she told him.

"Well, if you ever need more inspiration in the future, you just let me know," he told her with a teasing smile.

She nodded, feeling happy with the way everything was. She got back to her canvas after they kissed goodbye, and she had the art inspiration that she needed. Soon, her fingers worked in a dizzying way, moving about as she continued to smile. She thought about how intimate that action was, and she finally got fucked in her studio, something she so desperately wanted. Carli wouldn't mind trying this once again, and she wouldn't mind trying anal again and again in this studio.

The Stepmother's Love for Anal

Destiny loved anal, but her ex-husband never did it.

Of course, when she couldn't get it from him, she immediately went to her stepson, who was now not even a member of the family. Destiny married into the family for one reason, and one reason only: cold, hard cash. That meant that she now had a wonderful settlement, but she hated her love life with her ex. The truth was, they never did more than vanilla bullshit, and when Destiny said that she wanted to try anal, he was adamantly against it.

But, her stepson Frankie certainly loved it.

As she felt him kiss down her body, she soon shivered. She had the money now, but she also got the stepson. The truth was, Frankie and his father ended up having a huge fight, and the soon parted ways. Sure enough, he asked to come stay with her for a bit, since he was only 20 and needed to get on his feet. Destiny was fine with that, and they both agreed they wanted to continue this little shindig.

As he continued to tease her nipples with his tongue and fingers, she reached up, grasping a tuft full of blonde hair. That was another thing, her ex didn't have hair, and when she heard the groan from the other man's mouth, she felt a sense of excitement and need. She soon began to tug on the hair more and more, causing him to let out a series of moans and groans.

34

She smiled to herself, watching as he continued to move down towards her thick pussy, teasing the folds there.

"Fuck, you're so good," she said.

Frankie simply smiled and pushed a lubed finger into her. When did he lube up his finger, she didn't fucking know, but she didn't care as she felt the stretch against her body, the sudden need for more, so much fucking more, starting to drive her completely fucking mad.

His motions were very exact, and as he continued to move his fingers in and out of her pucker, teasing her clit with his tongue, she felt as if her entire body was at the mercy of this man, completely enthralled by the way he did this. His actions were skilled, way more skilled than the average man, and when she felt him add a second finger, diving his tongue in to tease that bundle of nerves within her, she immediately tensed up, screaming out loud, and the throes of her orgasm started to erupt. Of course, he licked all of this up with a fervency even she was surprised about, and when he pulled back, licking his lips in satisfaction, he looked at her with a smoldering glance, need obvious in his eyes.

"Fuck my ass," she said.

"Damn, you're desperate today Destiny," Frankie said.

"Because you're the best fuck I've got. You're so much better than your dad. He doesn't know how to treat a girl right in the bedroom," Destiny said.

That was met with a grunt of approval before he turned Destiny around, smacking her thick butt and causing her to let out a moan of satisfaction.

"You like that don't you?"

"Yes I fucking do," she told him.

"Well, there is more where that came from," he said.

Doggy style was the preferred method of choice for anal for Destiny, because he got in deep, and the penetration was amazing. As he pushed himself all the way in, destiny let out a groan of satisfaction, feeling his cock push all the way into her, filling her up. It was such a familiar feeling, and as he started to push himself in and out of her with the smallest of thrusts, Destiny lost her shit. She screamed out, tensing up with every single thrust, and soon, she felt him push in and out of her like a piston. Every single pistoned movement drove her mad, and when he started to push in deeper, his hands moved towards her clit, rubbing her with a fervency she never thought she'd get to enjoy. Destiny was grunting and groaning, only able to make those sounds and not much else.

"Yes, please fuck me. Please completely destroy my ass!" she cried out.

"You know I'lll do that for you baby," Frankie said.

He pulled her around, pressing his lips to her own in a passionate, needy kiss. As he did that, he pushed in deeper, his thrusts hitting that one spot, and that, combined with the clitoral stimulation was more than enough for destiny.

She screamed out, sounds that she normally didn't do in the past due to the fact that she needed to be quiet about this, but the fact that her ex husband isn't in the picture anymore allowed her to make the wanton noises she desired. She felt her entire body tighten, pleasure a big part of everything that was going through her head right now, and she soon came hard.

She then felt a couple more penetrative thrusts, and then, there was a groan. She looked up at Franky, and as he came, a look of complete satisfaction was present on his face. He looked at her, and soon, she smiled back.

"You good?"

"Oh I'm very good, you're certainly better than your father ever was, that's for sure," she said.

"Yeah, I'm glad about that. I heard he's getting remarried. Are you upset about that?"

Destiny laughed to herself, hearing how pathetic this guy was.

"Wow, so he kicks me to the corner and then goes for some other girl? What a fucking idiot. Not my problem though," she told him.

He laughed, looking at Destiny with an approving smile.

"Yeah, I don't blame you. he's definitely an idiot. But you have someone better now, right?"

"Course babe. Love you."

It was weird how that all happened, but destiny loved that she had a man ready to give her the anal pounding she wanted, and the fun that she desired.

Josh's First Time

Josh didn't expect his girlfriend Faye to agree to this, but as she sat there, naked and beautiful with her pussy spread, and her tiny little hole, he blushed.

"So how do you want to do this?" he asked.

"I wouldn't mind riding. I heard it hurts the least," she said.

Josh flushed at those words, listening to them and nodding.

"I can do that," he said.

Josh then spread her apart, already noticing how wet she was from when he ate her out and fucked her a little bit earlier. He almost came during then, but he wanted to try it in her ass. He soon pushed a finger in, pressing her legs up so that her hole was right there. He watched as the pucker resisted for a minute, but then as he pushed it in deeper and deeper, she then let out a small cry.

"Fuck," she said.

"I'm not hurting you, right?" he inquired.

"No, you're good. it's just...different that's all," she admitted.

Josh pushed the finger in deep, penetrating her, and as he looked over at her, he noticed that she was at first a bit pained, but then she relaxed. He pushed a second finger into her, letting his other hand that was free play with her nipples, and as he watched her, he noticed the need for more as she started to stare at him.

"Fuck," she said.

"You good there princess?" he asked.

"Yeah, I'm good," she said to him.

"Great. I'm going to continue."

Josh knew that he needed to take it slow, and as he pushed the second digit into Faye, earning a small moan of approval from her, he smiled, knowing that she went from disliking this, to enjoying the sensations. He began to thrust his fingers in and out of her, starting with the smallest of touches and then going a bit faster. After he was able to push a third finger in, he began to lick her clit, touching her there slightly as he continued the onslaught against her body.

"Holy shit," she muttered, tensing up at his words. He smiled, continually moving his fingers in a very dainty, but also in a way that made her feel good, manner. He watched as she went from being against every action to keening her body so that she could enjoy it. It was after the third finger that he felt she was ready.

He soon pushed his fingers out, earning a gasp from her, and soon, he started to move his hands towards the bottle of lube. With a shaky hand, he rubbed the contents on himself, and she soon looked at him.

Josh sat back, watching as Faye moved right over his cock, the hungry hole practically begging for him to completely push into. With a sigh, he did, and soon, he was all the way inside her tight pucker.

The sudden, overwhelming feeling of her hole taking him in drove Josh mad. He immediately felt the urge to slam down and fuck the shit out of her, but instead, he let her move her body up and down with small jerks, moaning in pleasure at the sensations that she felt. He looked up at her, and she gave him a reassuring smile.

"I'm good," she said.

"Great. I'm glad babe," he said.

She started moving a bit faster and faster, and as he watched her do this, he felt his own cock start to grow needier. He wanted to move her faster, but he wanted to make sure that she didn't get hurt. So he sat there, watching the show as she continued this, and it was then that, after a few more thrusts, she relaxed, looking at him.

"I want you to try," she said.

"What do you mean?" he inquired.

"I want you to...try pushing inside me. Fucking me. I want you to go harder," she told him with a flushed face.

This was the first time Josh saw his girlfriend so needy, and as he pulled back, he nodded at her.

"Well, I can definitely do that," he said with a smile.

She smiled back with a happy grin, and he soon grasped her hips, plunging his cock in deeper and deeper and controlling the thrusts.

This was better than he imagined! It was tight, so goddamn tight it drove him mad, and as he started to move himself up and down against her, watching with rapt eyes as she responded to his actions, he felt the urge to do more, so much more. He continued to thrust into her with a faster pace than he imagined he would get to try, and it was then when she started to move with him. Together, they thrust together, and it surprised Josh that she was getting off to this so readily. But then, after a few more thrusts, she soon tensed up, and Josh watched as she cried out loud, tensing up quite a bit as she soon came against him.

That was enough for Josh to let out a groan of pleasure, letting his body move against hers, and soon, as he pushed in, he moaned, emptying himself into her. It felt so right, so perfect, and then, after a few more thrusts, he pulled back and smiled at her.

"You good?" he asked.

"That was just...wow," she admitted, blushing madly.

"I take it that it's a good wow then," he teased.

"Yeah, a very good wow. I'd do it again if I could," she admitted.

Josh felt a strange sense of happiness as he heard those words. He knew for a fact that he would get a chance to do this again, and when he was here with her, he felt like he was enjoying this far more than he imagined he would get to.

It was the perfect moment, the opportunity he'd been waiting for, and he knew that with Faye by his side, happy to be fucked like this, he knew he'd get to do it again.

Anal on the Beach

"Are you sure you want to do this?" Danica asked, her naked backside looking perfect in the sand.

Ray knew though that this was the opportunity of a lifetime. Here they were, on a nude beach together that allowed for intimate activities, and he had a dream to take his girlfriend's anal virginity here. Danica had been practicing, as how she told him through sexts, but he never took it until the time was right.

"Yeah babe. I want to," he told her.

The blush on her face said it all, but Danica wasn't going to complain. Soon, she smacked her butt in a teasing manner, looking at him on all fours while she was on the towel.

"Then come here, take my ass," she replied, her voice a needy, smoldering tone that set Ray on fire.

His cock was aching, hard as a rock, and when he moved closer, letting his hands touch her fluffy, huge ass, he played with her pucker, realizing that she was partially prepared. He looked at her, and then she flushed.

"I was getting ready for this moment," she admitted.

"Then I guess that makes two of us," he teased as he pushed a finger in gently. The first two fingers went in with no problems, but Ray wanted to try something else.

He wanted to rim her.

He never got to do that before, but seeing the perfect little ass, the need in her eyes, and the way that her pucker was practically begging for him made him spread her cheeks, tongue diving straight into her ass to play with it. She immediately gasped at the strange and foreign feeling, and Ray wondered if she might say something. But then, she didn't, and Ray took this as a sign that she wanted more, and that's what he did.

His tongue dove in deep, teasing her ass, and when he saw her relax, moaning at the actions that he bestowed to her, he knew that he was at least doing something right. He continued to dine on her fine booty until she pulled back, flushing red.

"That's fine," she said.

"You good?" he asked.

"Yeah it's nice but...I really want your cock," she said.

Her naked backside was begging for it. Ray looked around, realizing that they were all alone. He could feel the breeze, smell the ocean, and look at his beautiful girlfriend as he did this. He shifted his body, taking his cock that was hard as a rock out of his swim trunks, and soon, he pressed into her.

The sound that came out of her mouth was that of a garbled scream, but also that of a moan of pleasure. He soon started to press in deeper, pushing all the way in to the hilt. He was balls deep in her ass, and he loved the feeling of it. He began to press against her, fucking her slowly at first to get a feeling for this, but then, she turned around, a look of desperation present in her eyes.

"Don't just fuck around here, fuck my ass so hard I'm seeing stars," she demanded.

He never expected to hear those words, but they were an impetus for him, and soon, he began to thrust in deeper and deeper, loving the delicious sounds that he heard, his body craving more from this beautiful woman. He started to fuck her faster and faster, getting in deep and penetrating her as such. She cried out, the excitement in her body, and the need in her eyes saying everything. He started to grab her hips, pushing all the way in and feeling her react to how deep his cock was getting.

He did look up at Danica a couple of times, but she seemed perfectly passive. As they continued to fuck though, she reached around, grabbing one of Ray's hands and putting it against her pussy.

"Rub me, I'm getting close," she said.

Those were the words that made Ray act immediately in instinct, pressing his hands there and rubbing her tight pussy with his fingers. He started to fuck her harder and harder, letting his cock push in deep, and it was then when she started to cry out, each and every single thrust driving her to the brink of insanity. Ray knew that if there was anyone around, they would've heard them, but they were all alone, and he knew for a fact that nobody cared what they did on the beach.

"I'm fucking close," he said.

"I am too."

After a few more thrusts, he reached inside, touching the bundle of nerves there. She screamed out, suddenly shaking at the feelings that she got, and it was then that, after a few more thrusts, she soon came hard. The tightness and the constriction was enough to drive Ray to the brink of insanity as well, and it was then when he pulled out, his cum spraying all over her ass.

He felt satisfied, his whole body shaking with delight. When he finished, he laid down on the sand, his shorts covered with both sand and a little bit of cum. When he looked at Danica, who seemed spent, he smiled.

"Did you know that?"

"Yes. It was the best thing. I want to have sex on the beach way more often now," she said with a smile on her face.

Ray took that as a good sign, and when he reached in to give her a kiss, he beamed right back.

"Well, I guess that makes two of us then. I think it's safe to say that we are definitely going to come back here and do this again."

that was an amazing first time anal experience for both of them, and when Ray realized what he just did, he knew that he wanted to do it again and again with this woman, for it was the best thing he experienced in a long time.

Office Anal Fun

It was a late night and when Laura called Dylan to come over for a romp, she wanted something else. When he opened the door, he saw Laura there, clad in nothing but stockings, a garter belt, and her suit jacket and shirt. But, Laura was already planning for something more, and as she shook her ass in the most tantalizing manner, he looked at her, his cock hard as a rock.

"You want in on this?" she said, wiggling her hips and smirking at the other.

Dylan immediately reached over, spreading her ass cheeks and diving his tongue into her, lapping at her pucker and her pussy. When he did this, Laura immediately gasped, feeling both the stimulation from her pussy, and from her needy ass.

She already did the prepping earlier, and when he pushed his tongue into her hole, she immediately shivered, crying out loud and immediately gasping in complete and utter pleasure. She felt like it was heaven on earth as he did this, the small touches driving her completely insane. As he continued to push his tongue in deeper, she pushed her ass closer to his face, smothering him with it.

This was amazing, but then, Dylan pushed two fingers in, letting his tongue play with her folds from over near her clit. She gasped, feeling everything start to change, and soon, she began to feel the buildup from her orgasm. He continued his motions, getting her close, but then, he moved back, causing Laura to groan.

"Don't worry babe, I'm about to give you everything that you want," he told her with a smile.

She smiled back at him, and that's when he pushed his cock against her cheeks, freeing it from the confines first and then pressing the tip against her hole. He pushed in, causing her to let out a sudden gasp in pleasure at the sensation of him filling her up. When he got all the way in, he looked at her, giving her a passionate, needy kiss before he started to move his cock.

At first, the motions were slow, but with the way her ass was positioned on the desk, and the way his cock was angled, it felt amazing. She was so full, so stuffed, that every single motion drove her completely mad. He continued to thrust in deep, enjoying the tightness of her ass.

Dylan loved her ass. It was something that he truly did enjoy on Laura. Sure, they were partners, but they did sometimes have personal romps in the office after hours. Laura usually was the top dog, but when it came to the bedroom, Dylan knew immediately what to do to turn her on, and everything that she enjoyed.

"You like that you dirty little slut," he said, slapping her ass cheek hard and causing a moan to emit from her lips.

"Ahh yes! I love it," she told him.

"Good. You're going to keep taking my cock however I want to give it to you," he said.

Of course, Laura didn't want him to stop. In fact, she scooted her body over towards the middle, causing him to move onto the desk.

"Fuck me on this desk," she said with a demanding tone of voice.

He didn't need to be told twice. Suddenly, he moved up, holding her hips as he thrust in deep, penetrating her harder than ever before. He began to watch as she sat there, desire and need growing in her body as she continued to feel him penetrate her harder and harder. Everything was so perfect, so nice, and as she felt him continue this, she could feel his hands move up, penetrating her pussy with the deepest of touches while he fucked her ass.

He tweaked her nipples too as he continued to thrust, feeling her gasp and tighten up as a result of that. She then felt everything immediately go white, and when he pushed against that bundle of nerves, she immediately gasped, feeling everything stop.

When she came, she started to moan out loud, feeling everything grow more and more intense. It was then when she came hard, feeling like she just hit the jackpot. As she finally finished, he pulled back, grasping her hips hard once again and pushing as deep as he could with all his force.

It felt like heaven when he felt his cock begin to twitch, and when he came with a groan he immediately filled her ass up. He wanted to make sure that he got it in as deep as he could, and when he finished the last of his thrusts, he pulled back, smiling in excitement.

"You good?" he asked her.

Laura was down with her ass planted up in the air, feeling the sudden shock of everything as it came to her.

"Yeah. That was...truly amazing," she said.

"Good. I'm glad that you liked that," he said, giving her ass one last smack before pulling back, eying her body one last time. If he wasn't so tired, he'd consider fucking her once again, but he was definitely not able to keep his eyes open.

"Do you need to be walked home?" Dylan asked.

"Nah, I should be good. Besides, if people know about us, I think it may cause a bit of drama, so I'd rather not have that," she admitted.

Laura wished they could be a couple, but she knew the risks. They were both highly-trained business people, and they both knew what would happen if they continued on this route. It would end up being a problem, that's for sure.

"That's true. I'm glad that I have this though. Even if it's just temporary, I'm glad I still have your cute ass that is fun to fuck," he said.

She smiled, and the two of them shared one last kiss before they pulled away, going to their own lives once again, until the next time they needed one another for a release.

Anal Fun when the Store is Closed

It was 10 pm, which meant that the only two people that were here were Lisa, and of course her coworker Carl. The two of them were close, closer than most would ever imagine, but of course neither of them would ever let anyone, let alone corporate, know about that. If someone found out about them, it could mean trouble, especially when it came to what they liked to do here.

What they liked to do was make out against the counter, both of them feeling the pleasure of one another's lips and their tongues as they continued to kiss one another in a passionate manner. Lisa was enthralled by all of this, her body aching for him, and she knew that Carl wanted this too. As they continued to make out, he pushed his hands to the edge of her pants, undoing them and pulling them off. They were right near one of the shelves that was sturdy enough for them to hold themselves up, but also not one that was uncomfortable.

As Carl started to press his fingers against the obvious wet spot in her pants, he heard Lisa let out a moan of desire. He smiled, looking at her and kissing her once again.

"You like this?"

"Fuck yes I do. I want this," she said.

The other smiled, and soon, he started to press his hands towards the edge of the waistband of her pussy, pushing the

54

garment down along with her jeans. He started to press two fingers into her, like how he always did, and with small, succulent ouches, he began to lightly finger her, enough that it drove her completely mad with pleasure as she felt her body cling to his own.

"Fuck," she said with a moan.

"You like that babe?"

"Yeah, but I want it in the ass tonight," she said.

He looked at her surprised by this, and then she pointed to the obvious bottle of lube that was sitting there on the shelf. He smiled as he grabbed the contents and poured it on his hands, looking at her with desire in his eyes.

"Well, I guess somebody wants this then."

As if on cue, he started to push a finger against the edge of her ass, penetrating her pucker in a ready manner. She immediately groaned, realizing and feeling the penetrative actions that came from this. She immediately felt the heavenly actions that came from this, and as he continued to push his hands deeper and deeper into both her holes, she felt as if she was losing her mind.

She continued to move her hips up to the edge of his fingers, practically begging for him to continue these actions, and then, after a few more thrusts, he added in two fingers to each hole, feeling her relax to the touch. He continued the actions, noticing the desire in her eyes.

"I want it now," she said.

"Alright princess," he teased. But then, he pushed his hands up and grasped her backside, touching the round orbs. They felt perfect in his hands, and as he felt her squirm to his touch, he immediately watched as she soon relaxed, feeling as if everything was driving her mad. He then moved his cock slowly into her, bracing her hip as he penetrated her deeply.

The sensation of this was almost too much to bear, and when he finally got all the way in, he immediately watched as she tensed up, feeling the effects of everything as he began to move his cock in and out slowly. The fact that he was bracing her like this as he continued to move himself in and out of her ass, feeling the tenseness of her body as he continued to penetrate deep into her. The feeling of this was far too much, and soon, as he began to feel more and more of this, he soon tensed up, and that's when he started to move his cock as fast as he could into her.

He could hear her squirm and moan in response as he continued his onslaught against her tight ass. The feeling of the tightness, the action that he took, the sheen of sweat that was against her body, and the feeling of her fluffy butt cheeks as he continued to fuck her mercilessly drove him completely insane. It was like heaven to him, and then after a few more thrusts he could feel his body getting close.

It was then when he moved his hand that wasn't holding her up to her clit, teasing it slightly, and then after a few more thrusts, he watched as she screamed out, tensing up and then relaxing as the feeling of her orgasm completely destroyed her. He watched with a smile on his face as he continued to push his cock in and out of her, and then, after a few more thrusts, he soon tensed up, groaning as he spilled himself all the way into her.

He could feel his cock emptying out, and she gasped as he felt his seed push all the way into her. It was magical, and she definitely didn't mind the fact that he was enjoying this just as much as she was. After he pulled away and let her down easy, she gasped, feeling the sudden shock of being on the ground wash over her.

"Wow, that was something," she admitted.

"Sure was," he said, smiling at her.

"That was just...wow. Amazing," she admitted.

"Yeah, I enjoyed that. Plus, we've been due for a romp like that, right?" he told her.

"You're telling me," she replied.

They smiled at one another, kissing once again. It was the beginning of another long night of cleaning between them, but the fact that they had each other was enough for her. She certainly wouldn't complain, and she knew that he enjoyed this as well.

Barn Anal Adventures

Doing it in the barn was something that Abby wanted to try, but getting her boyfriend Tyler to agree to something like this was another trial within itself. She watched as he looked at her with abject confusion as she pulled him inside. They did mess around a little bit in the barn, a place that she liked to spend time with her boyfriend, but rarely did they get past third base with this.

But then, as they made out, and clothes came off, Abby had an idea. She looked at Tyler, smiling as she fished out the bottle of lube.

"Hey Tyler, have you ever thought about putting it in my butt?" she asked.

Tyler looked at her as if she had three heads for a second.

"N-no! I never have!"

"Really now? Even though you totally could?" she said with a simpering smile.

Tyler blushed, but then he took a deep breath, steeling himself before he spoke.

"I haven't. I mean, I think it might be nice, but I'm not totally sure," he said.

"Well, why don't we try it? I've done a little bit of anal play, but I haven't done much besides that," she said.

Tyler blushed. He always wanted to try it in a sense, but he didn't want to ask Abby about it.

"I mean...sure. I'lll do it," he said.

Abby smiled, feeling his hands move up towards her backside, and as he uncapped the bottle of lube, he pushed the contents onto his fingers. As he did that, Abby pulled his fly and zipper open, and when he looked at her with confusion, she simply smiled.

"I want to fuck you while you prepare me," she said.

Tyler was too shocked for words, but when she moved down onto his cock, pressing herself onto there, he immediately groaned. He started to rock in and out of her, moaning at the sensation that he felt. He didn't expect this to feel so good, but here he was, penetrating one hole while preparing another, and when he pushed the second finger into there, he immediately watched as she started to tense up, moaning out loud at the feeling of both her holes being stimulated.

Tyler was amazed at all that she could take. When he inserted a third finger, he watched as she immediately gasped, holding him as she continued to ride his cock. For Tyler, the penetration was practically too much to bear, and then, after another thrust, he pulled out, gasping.

"Okay please, I really need to be in you right now, because if we don't do it now, I'm going to cum in the wrong hole," Tyler admitted. His voice was hesitant, his mind racing and his head spinning at the sensations that he was failing.

Abby simply smiled, pushing her butt against the head of his cock, looking at him with a dark smile.

"Well don't worry, I'lll make sure you're definitely taken care of," she said.

Tyler didn't know what he was getting into, but when he felt Abby press down onto his member, filling her up with his cock, he immediately gasped. It was so much tighter than he thought it would be, and when he felt her take him all the way in, he thought he was going to lose his fucking mind.

He then watched as she, with a devilish smile, began to rock her hips up and down on him. The smallest of sensations was enough to drive him insane, and she soon moved her body up and down, faster and faster, the desire for more growing within both of them. Tyler could feel his entire body losing control, he could feel everything start to become completely out of his element. He watched as she started to thrust in and out, and then, after a few more thrusts, he then watched as she tensed up, and he began to feel his whole cock just practically burst with need.

"Fuck. I think I'm going to cum," she said.

That was all that he needed to know. He watched as she, after a few more thrusts, began to cry out, touching her clit with a few motions but then feeling the throes of her orgasm as she soon came hard.

The tightness that he felt was practically overwhelming. For Tyler, he knew that his girlfriend was tight, which was one of the marvels of her, but her ass was a whole new world. He gripped her cheeks, pushing down against there one last time before he soon cried out. He then relaxed, and as he came hard inside of her, she shivered at the sensation of the cum hitting every part of her inside. She shivered, and when he finished up, he pulled out, looking at her with a smile on his face.

"Like that princess?" he asked.

"Yeah. I did," she said, her breathing heavy and her body aching.

He pulled her off, cuddling her in his arms. The hay was starting to feel a little bit scratchy, and Abby immediately placed her clothes back on. Tyler tucked himself away in his pants once again, and then, after a few moments, looked at her and smiled.

"You enjoy that?"

"Yeah. That was amazing," she said.

"Good. I mean, I didn't expect your ass to be that tight, that's for sure," he said.

Abby blushed, but then, after a brief second, she spoke.

"So you want to try it again?" she asked.

"Perhaps. Maybe we should try it in the barn once more. People don't come out here, and I think it's pretty nice," he said.

"Yeah, it's definitely something that I don't mind," she said.

The two of them smiled to one another, the excitement that grew within them driving them both mad. Abby loved the way everything transpired, but at the same time, she wondered how much more fun she could have with her ass. What was next? What would she do now? She certainly wanted to explore more of this, and with the boyfriend she adored as well.

Anal as Payment

"Shit, I broke it!" Camie cried out as she looked at the contents.

It was then when she heard the footsteps of the mysterious man, the guy whose house she was cleaning. She gulped, realizing that this wasn't going to be good, it wasn't going to be good at all.

Camie realized just what was going to happen. She probably would get sent home, but when her boss Leo came in, inspecting the area, he noticed the vase.

"You broke it!" he said.

"I'm sorry, I was just trying to clean and--"

"You know that's a precious vase, right? You can't do that," he said.

Camie blushed, but she didn't know what her punishment should be.

"What can I do? I mean, will you dock my pay, take more money out of my paycheck, make me work extra--"

"Your ass," Leo simply said.

She looked at him as if he had three heads.

"Excuse me?"

"I want your ass," he said.

She immediately realized what was going on. She soon turned around, looking at him with a flushed face as she showed her backside. His hands moved towards her skirt, pushing it up to reveal her plump ass cheeks. After a couple of smacks, causing her to let out a shudder of pleasure, he then pulled away, caressing the flesh there.

"I want to fuck this," he said.

Camie never did anal before. Would it hurt? She looked at Leo, the dashing brunette making her do stupid shit. But then, he moved his hands to his pockets, grabbing some silicone-based lube that he had around.

"I always keep this around for safekeeping," he explained.

She couldn't believe he was that prepared, but then, as he uncapped the bottle, pushing the contents onto his fingers and looked at her, he smiled a smirk that made her body hot.

"Don't worry princess, I'lll take good care of you," he said.

What did he plan on doing? It was then when he pushed his hands against the tip of her pucker, and while she expected this at first to hurt, she didn't expect it to feel so...nice. She looked at him, and he soon smiled, letting his hands move towards her entrance and penetrating her deep.

The sensation of her ass being fucked immediately drove her insane. It felt so different, and even though it was just her fingers, it was a sensation that felt better than she expected it to. She soon felt him add a second finger, stretching her out, and the first thing that she noticed about all of this, was the fact that he was actually very soft with his touches, in a way that was almost surreal in a sense.

"Fuck," she said with a moan, immediately letting her ass move against his fingers. As he did this, he smirked, watching the sensation.

"You like this, don't you?"

"Yes," she breathed out, feeling like everything was driving her mad.

He continued to penetrate her, first with two, and then with three, and then, as if on cue he pulled them out, teasing the very edge of her entrance before he soon unzipped his pants. She didn't know what she was going to feel, but then, when she felt the big, meaty organ penetrate her deeply, she felt as if she was losing her mind.

It was super tight, and she felt like she was practically being split open. She watched as he looked at her, sliding each inch in with small movements. She felt like her entire body was being filled up, and it was a different sensation that she was not used to. She then started to feel him push all the way in, getting straight into her completely, and when he was finally in, he waited a minute before moving.

Instead of it hurting though, it felt good. It was a strange kind of pleasure, and as he continued to fuck her tight little hole, Camie felt the need for more. More was something that she never thought she'd want to feel, but he was so good, and the tightness was enough to drive her insane.

He moved his cock faster and faster, in and out of her with movements that surprised her. He was so good, and everything was making her feel like her entire body was losing control. She watched as he continued to grab her ass, smacking it as the sounds of smacking that came from his cock filled the room.

She cried out, gasping in pleasure as he did this, and then, after a few more thrusts, he soon tensed up, and that's when he did it.

He spilled his contents into her, the heat from his cock and cum immediately making her shiver. He penetrated her a couple more times, enjoying the way that she felt, before he pulled out with a pop. He simply zipped his pants up once again before he spoke to her.

"That is your punishment for breaking the vase. I hope you never do that again," he said.

The fact that it was all that he said before walking off surprised Camie, but then she felt that it wasn't necessarily the worst punishment that she was dealt. In truth, it was a punishment she wouldn't mind trying once again, one that involved her experiencing that same feeling that he gave to her before.

Maybe it wasn't a punishment, but in fact something good that she would love to experience again and again. Maybe next time she could make the punishment even heavier, and she could get fucked even harder than she had ever been fucked in the past.

The idea made her almost want to knock something off again, that's for sure.

The Maid's Request

When Ellie went into Ben's office, she expected him to give her the cleaning duties for the day. Working for a rich businessman occasionally had the perks that she enjoyed such as lots of money, but he was a bit of a loose cannon when it came to what he wanted. Sometimes he liked to make strange requests, and when she got to the office, she heard the first request that surprised her in a long time.

"I heard that you haven't been cleaning as fast as usual," he said.

"I mean...I've been trying," she admitted.

"Trying isn't good enough Ellie. I'm going to have to punish you for this," he snapped.

How was he going to punish her? She looked at him, unsure of what he meant by that, but then he gestured to her backside.

"Turn, lay on that chaise lounge with your ass up in the air," he demanded.

Ellie followed instructions, slightly worried about what this might entail, but instead of something bad, she felt warm hangs rub her thighs, getting towards the lower part of her cheeks, and soon, she immediately tensed up, feeling a strange comfort in this touch. He then smacked it, causing a small moan to escape her mouth.

"Good girl. You like it when I spank your ass?"

"Yes sir," she said, slightly shaky from the shock of the motion.

"Good. If you want, I can make you feel good. Plus, it would be a fitting reward for you, and a good punishment too," he said.

Ellie hesithated, unsure of what to say in response, but then she nodded.

"Yes. Please fuck my ass," she said.

She knew Ben for a long time, and the fact that he was willing to do something such as this surprised her. But, with a grin he moved his hands to a bottle of lube that was on the counter, undoing the contents and pouring them onto his fingers. He slipped her panties to the side, pushing a digit into her, and when he penetrated her initially, it felt a bit strange but at the same time, a bit pleasurable.

She never expected to get fucked like this, but here she was, being penetrated by her boss, the man that she did have a small crush on, so it made everything even better.

After a brief moment or so, he then started to push his fingers deeper and deeper, adding in a second finger and rubbing her clit. Her panties were already soaked, and as he continued the motions, he smiled.

"You're already so fucking wet. Does me fingering your ass turn you on that much?" he asked.

"Yes," she cried out, feeling her body shake with pleasure.

"Oh then, I'm glad that you enjoy it," he told her.

He began to thrust the two fingers in deeper and deeper, and it was then when he finally pushed a third in, causing her to let out a small moan of pleasure and desire. After a brief moment, he then pulled his fingers out, and she heard the sound of a zipper being undone, and then the sound of a groan of relief.

He was going to fuck her ass. Ellie did dream of this moment, for she wanted him to do this to her. But, she never expected him to go this far. He soon spread her apart, and that's when she felt his cock right near her pucker.

She shivered, and when he pushed in she let out a small groan of both shock and pleasure as he began to move himself deep within her. He watched as she gasped, feeling her entire body become enraptured in the pleasure. He was soon all the way in, and when he got inside, he looked at her, and she soon shivered.

"You want more princess?"

"Yes please," she said.

He then started to move his cock in and out of her, starting with slow thrusts to get her used to it, but then the thrusts became longer, and much deeper than she expected. She soon began to shiver, tensing up and moaning in desire as she felt him push his dick all the way in, groaning before he started to work at a more forceful pace. After a brief moment, she could tell that he was getting desperate, the thrusts becoming almost too fast for her to keep up, and as she felt him hit that spot each time, that strange spot that made her cry out, she wanted more.

He slipped his hands to her front, fingering her as he continued this, and it was then that, after a brief moment, she soon cried out, feeling every single fiber in her body start to go insane at the sensations. She then started to cry out, and she soon shivered, moaning in pleasure as she came hard against him. She could feel her ass squeezing his cock, the moan of approval that he uttered immediately turning her on.

"Fuck," he said to her.

It was then after a couple more final thrusts, he let out a moan, and he soon came hard, penetrating himself deep into her. He watched as she shivered throughout her body as he released deep within her. When he was done, pulled out, tucking himself back in.

"That should be enough of a reward and punishment right?" he said.

"Yes master," she said.

"Good. Well, I guess that means I'lll get to have fun with that cute little ass again in the future if you decide to disobey me," he said.

When she heard those words, she immediately realized that he did want to do this again, that he was desperate for her ass. She wanted his cock inside of her once again, and as she left his office, she smiled, remembering that she could always disobey orders once again and get that same punishment that she knew she wanted, and the one that she craved more than she had ever before.

The Boss's Need

When Vicky heard that her boss George needed some relief, she thought that as her secretary, she would just be moving to him and taking over a few of the functions of the business. But no, when he told her that he wanted her to wear this ultra-short secretarial garb after hours, she was definitely not expecting what would happen next.

But here she was, dressed in a skirt that was short, and a jacket with only a mere bra underneath. When she got in there, George smiled, and he soon spoke.

"Seems like you took my offer," he said.

"Well you said you were offering me a promotion, and I really want it," she said.

"How much do you want it?"

She hesithated, unsure of what to even think what it came to that.

"I don't know what you mean?"

"What I mean is, are you willing to do anything that I request?" he inquired.

She didn't imagine it would be anything weird, so she nodded.

"Good. Get on the desk with your ass hanging out in the air," he uttered.

She looked at him with complete surprise, unsure of what to make of any of this, but then, after a brief moment, she did as she was told. The skirt was already riding up, exposing the thong that she had on.

"Good girl. You know, you have the best as of all of my employees, and I'm very happy that you took my offer," he said.

He gave her ass a hard smack, causing her to let out a gasp of both pain, and slight pleasure.

"Really now?"

"Yes. I really like your butt, and I've wanted to get some relief for a bit. So, what do you say, I take care of that ass, we both get off, and you get the promotion," he sthated.

Vicky realized just what he wanted. He wanted to fuck her ass. Sure, she would prefer that over her pussy, but even she was surprised by the request he uttered.

"Umm, sure," she said.

"Good. I'm glad you're as interested as I am," he said with a purr.

He smacked her ass a couple more times, earning small gasps from her, and soon, he moved to a drawer within his desk, fiddling with some lube that he had on hand.

"Never know when this might come in handy," he said.

He also had something else in his hands. A bullet vibrator. He settled the vibrator into her pussy, pressing in deep, and then, after a brief moment, he then pushed his first finger in.

The stimulation from the toy was enough to drown out the sudden shock that came from the fingers within her ass. She definitely didn't know what would happen next, or even what to do, but then, he pushed another finger deep into her, causing her to let out another cry of pleasure. He continued to push the digits in and out of her, making her whimper with pleasure.

He then started to push the fingers in and out, causing her to let out a series of small moans and groans of pleasure, her entire body experiencing a strange feeling a pleasure that she was definitely not used to. sure, she had sex in the past, but this was different. It never felt like this, but then, as he continued to penetrate her deeper and deeper, with the toy being teased as well, Vicky realized something.

She wanted more.

Her body ached for more. She hadn'thad dick in a long time, and the fact that he was giving her this made her shiver with delight. He began to push his fingers inside, adding a third for good measure, and that's when she looked at him, the need obvious in her eyes.

"Give me your cock. Please," she said.

"My, ever so needy kitten," he said.

"I just...really want to feel good," she said.

"Well, I'lll make sure that you feel utterly amazing," he said to her.

It was then when she felt him move his hands towards the edge of the toy, pushing it right up against her clit and the other hole before he unzipped his pants, lubing up his cock and getting ready to spread her cheeks. When he inserted himself into her, he did it with a slow motion, but it was enough to drive her utterly mad with pleasure.

"Fuck! Yes," she told him.

He smiled at her, pushing his cock in deeper and then letting it stay there for a moment. She did admit that it hurt a little bit, but then, after a moment, he began to thrust inside of her, causing her to let out a series of whimpers of both pleasure, and slight shock. It was tighter than she managed to feel before, and it did have a tightness she wasn't used to, but she also really enjoyed it.

George was going to town on her ass, moving as fast as he possibly could into her tight ass, enjoying the sounds that she made as he did this. He continued to smirk, the pleasure from all of this driving both of them mad. It was then that, after a few more thrusts, he soon started to increase the pace, and when he finally did, he pushed in deep, pressing the toy up, and they both came together.

The feeling of the cum in her ass felt nice, and she felt like she was experiencing something that was better than anything she had ever felt before. When he finished, he pulled his cock out, and when he looked at her, he noticed that she was grinning.

"You like that?"

"Yeah. Did I get the promotion?"

There was a smirk on his face, and after he kissed her, he nodded.

"Of course. You've managed to get the top promotion this month," he said.

Vicky was happy about that, and she wondered if he would do this again. She definitely wouldn't mind making her boss happy once more.

The Roommate's Dilemma

When Regina came in and saw her roommate Ricky masturbating, at first she was a little bit embarrassed. She didn't mean to walk in on him in the living room, masturbating to some chick taking a dick in her ass.

"Oh sorry!" he said.

"No it's my fault!" Regina said, immediately flushing and trying to shuffle away.

The awkward tensions that were there seemed to linger, and for Regina, she felt a strange urge. After everything was all said and done, Ricky looked at her.

"I didn't mean to do that," he said.

"No it's okay. Besides, there was something about it that kind of...interested me," she admitted.

He looked at her, and then, she took a deep breath, blushing as she spoke.

"The truth is...I kind of want to try anal with you. Since you like it so much. And I mean, we kind of do have the friends with benefits thing going on and--"

"Are you sure Regina," Ricky asked, and she soon nodded.

"Yeah. I'm sure," she admitted.

He then looked at her, smiling as he gave her a passionate kiss.

"Then I guess we can say it's worth a try," he told her with a smile on his face.

Regina wondered what was going to happen, but then, she was brought to the bedroom. They began to kiss with a fervency, and soon, their clothes came off. Ricky played with her breasts, teasing the large orbs, and she stroked his cock to hardness, feeling him moan in pleasure. They did play around, and Regina felt wetter than ever. It was then when Ricky looked at her, and then he spoke.

"So you cool with me doing this still?"

"I really want to try this," she admitted, blushing madly at the words that she uttered. It wasn't a lie, that's for sure.

Ricky smiled, and then, he started to grab the lube that he was using earlier to masturbate. He then spread her legs apart, teasing her pucker with his fingers. His tongue went towards her clit, teasing it there, and as he continued the motions, Regina began to moan.

"This is..pretty good," she said.

"Yeah, it's nice," he said, letting his fingers dance within her. She moaned, feeling the sudden urge for more begin to flood over her. She watched as he inserted another finger, his tongue and free hand teasing her body so that she was relaxed, and Regina was definitely that and so much more.

She loved every sensation that he was giving to her, and then, after a few more moments, he inserted a third finger, causing her to let out a sudden gasp of pleasure.

"You good?" he asked.

"Yeah. More than good. I'm definitely enjoying this," she admitted.

"Good. I'm glad then," he said with a smile.

He started to move his fingers in and out, stretching her once more before he slipped them away. She heard the sound of the lube bottle being uncapped again, and then, he pulled her into his arms, holding her there as he lightly thrust down.

The sudden breach made Regina scream, but she trusted Ricky, or she knew that he wasn't doing this just for himself, but also for her. He then pushed all the way in, and when she heard that needy, wanton groan, she knew that he was enjoying this just as much as she was.

He began to thrust in and out with the smallest of motions, each and every single movement generating pleasure on all fronts from both of them. It was almost mind-blowing how good it was, and as she felt him penetrate her deeper, she could feel herself wanting more. She met his thrusts with her own ass, feeling how tight and arousing it was, and it was then when she started to meet his own thrusts, her butt hitting his cock with a force that was unlike anything he imagined. He immediately groaned, each and every single motion driving him completely crazy, and then, after a few moments, she grasped her hips, pushing down on them and penetrating the area as deep as he could go.

The force of this drove her insane, and it was then after a moment or so she tensed up, screaming out loud as she felt her body ride out the orgasm. She felt like she was experiencing little taste of heaven, and as she felt him push himself deep into her once again, he then, after a few more thrusts, grabbed her ass, plunging as deep as he could before he came in her ass.

The sudden feeling of this shocked her more than anything. She didn't expect it to feel so...good in a sense. She thought it was going to be gross, but the feeling of this was a maddening one, one that drove her slowly to the brink of insanity, to enjoy the moment that she shared with her roommate.

The two of them stayed like this for a moment, basking in the feeling of pleasure before he pulled out. She laid down on the bed, cum trickling out of her ass, and when she looked at him, she smirked.

"Was that everything you imagined it to be?" she asked.

"Yes, that's for sure," he said to her.

She smiled, the excitement and the pleasure that she felt immediately exciting her more than anything else. She then watched as he looked at her, and for a moment, she considered asking him what was next. She wondered what now, but then, he leaned in, holding her close and stroking her hair.

"You know, I've thought about...doing things with you before, and the fact that we were able to this time...well it felt nice," he said.

"That's true," she admitted.

"I would love to do this again. doesn't have to be just anal either," he replied.

She smiled back, the excitement driving her body forward and hugging him. She wanted this too, and as they stayed there, she wondered indeed what was next for both of them.

Butt Fun at the Campsite

Hannah didn't expect her boyfriend Robert to want to go camping, but here they were, out in the middle of nowhere at a campsite, and they were in the tent cuddling. The night sounds were relaxing to Hannah, and when she looked at Robert, she felt a strange sense of happiness.

Robert was the man she'd fallen for, the one that she was madly in love with, but when he looked at her, she noticed that he had another look in his eyes, a look of something more.

The need for her.

The two of them started to kiss with a fervency that she was used to, one that she definitely enjoyed. But it was then, after a moment or so, that he pulled away, flushing as he looked at her.

"By the way babe, I've wanted to try something," he said to her.

"What is it?" she inquired, a bit surprised by this.

"Do you...want to try it in the butt?" he asked.

Hannah didn't know what to say. She did want to, but she wasn't prepared, and she didn't know if he was either.

"I'm not sure, I mean, I'm not prepared for that," she said.

"Well, I did bring a few things," he replied.

He brought forth a butt plug and some lube, and when she saw that, her eyes widened.

"Are you sure?" she asked.

"Damn sure. I really want to try this babe, that is if you're down," he said to her.

She listened to him, and as she looked at him, she immediately nodded.

"I'lll do it," she said.

She then moved her body so that it was down on the sleeping mattress they blew up. They made out, and slowly but surely clothes were being ripped off. Robert was gentle with his touches, caressing her inner folds before diving into her pussy with his tongue and fingers. Each and every single motion was enough to drive her mad, and with every single touch, she knew that she was definitely loving this more and more than she thought she would. She certainly felt some excitement, and it was then when she felt him move a finger towards her ass, touching the pucker with a massaging motion before he slipped it into her. She gasped, feeling it completely fill her up, and it was then when, she felt him push his fingers in deeper and deeper, making her practically scream out loud and in pleasure.

"Fuck," she told him.

He nodded, moving his fingers in a skillful manner. He wanted to make sure that hewasn'thurting her, and with every single motion, every single passing second, she felt as if there was something bigger coming.

Each finger felt like a heavenly stretch that she enjoyed far more than she cared to admit, and it was after she had three fingers inside that she soon tensed up, and that's when she told him she was ready.

"Let's...do this," she said.

Robert looked at her, feeling how wet she was down there, and how she was experiencing everything that was going on, but then, after a brief moment, he then pulled back, looking at her.

"Do you want to ride or..."

"I wouldn't mind doggy-style," she admitted with a flush.

He blushed back, surprised she wanted that, but then, he started to pull back, lubing himself up as she got on her hands and knees, her ass hanging out there in front of him like a fruit that was begging to be picked.

When he pushed inside, at first it was tight. It felt almost too tight for her to have it in there, but then after he finished up and stopped, it became almost comfortable, and when she felt him sink into there, she couldn't believe how nice it was.

She felt like everything was driving her mad, and then, after a few more thrusts, she soon started to tense up, and that's when she began to feel him move in and out of her slowly. He took it easy, letting his hands move towards her breasts, fondling them as he began to penetrate her slowly. Each touch sent shivers down her spine, made her lose control, and everything began to go white.

She loved the strange feeling of need that came from this, the feeling of him completely penetrating her every fiber of her body. As he began to fuck her harder, she began to cry out with each thrust, and she was very happy that they were in the middle of the forest, or this would be hella awkward.

He started to thrust deeper and deeper, each one completely decimating her and making her want more. It was then when, with one last final thrust, she soon screamed out, everything going blank as she came hard, feeling the throes of her orgasm as it happened.

She felt like a million dollars, and it was then when, after a few more thrusts, Robert cried out as well, a manly groan filling the tent, and he came inside of her. It was a relieving feeling that coursed through her, and when she felt the way his cum filled her up, it made her want to have more.

He finished up with a couple final thrusts before he pulled away, looking at her with expectant eyes.

"You good?" he asked.

"Really good. Holy fuck," she said.

"I take it that's exactly what you needed," he admitted.

"Yeah. It honestly was. That was...wow," she said.

The two of them embraced one another in the tent under the stars, both of them enjoying the presence of one another, and both of them ready to do this again sometime in the future. It was a first time that she enjoyed, and she knew that Robert loved it too.

She definitely wouldn't mind going camping more often if it meant something like this.

The Sugar Daddy's Request

"What do you mean?" Veronica asked, looking at her sugar daddy Kain. She had been in the business of being sugared for a long time, about a year and a half now, and while the money was amazing, she never got asked this request before. Sure, sex was part and parcel of the job, but this...was different.

"I want your ass baby girl," Kain her sugar daddy said with a purr.

Veronica flushed, but she certainly wasn't against the idea of it. In fact, she was morbidly curious about it, and when she looked at him, she soon spoke.

"You mean like...you want to fuck my ass?"

"That's what I want. Plus, if you do it well, I'll give you something a little extra, if that's what you want that is," he said.

She blushed, but then she nodded.

"I wouldn't mind that. In all honesty," she said.

"Good. Well get on your hands and knees baby girl, and I'lll take care of you tonight," he said.

Veronica was used to sexual favors, but this was new to her. Though, it was strange because she wanted to learn more about this. It struck a sense of morbid curiosity within her, and as she laid there with her ass up in the air, she watched as he smiled at her, a devilish grin that said everything.

"You have such a nice ass babygirl," he said.

"Thank you," she said, flushing as he touched her body with the subtlest of touches. He began with the little touches that went from her thighs, and then up to her ass, cupping it for a second before he delivered three soft spanks to her. She let out a soft moan of approval, her entire body moaning in response to the man's actions. She loved this, and as he continued to slap her, she wondered if this was what he meant by this.

But then, he moved his hands to her panties, rubbing her there, and as he did that, she let out a slight gasp of shock, her entire body immediately responding to this. She wanted more, and as she felt him press his fingers there a couple of explorative ones went to her pucker, touching it there.

What Veronica didn't expect, was for it to feel this good. She soon felt him press his fingers into her pussy, her entire body reacting to this as he pushed one singular finger into her ass. She gasped, feeling the slight approval of the touch ghost through her body. He continued to press his fingers with soft touches against her ass, watching as she squealed and moved around with delight.

"I didn't even know you were into that. Little slut," he said, giving her a smack on the butt.

She gasped, feeling like everything was about to get better and better. He was using one hand to smack, and the other was teasing her pussy and ass with fingers and rubbing. All of this felt lovely, and as he continued this, Veronica wanted more.

She never experienced this need before. It felt so good, and when he pushed three fingers into there, she loved the familiar sensation of tightness that seemed to come over her. He began to move his hands over towards her ass, teasing it slightly once more before he pulled away. It was then when she heard the belt come undone and his fly unzip, and that's when she realized that he was indeed going to fuck her ass.

Would this hurt? She honestly didn't know, and it was then when she started to feel him move his hands towards her ass cheeks, cupping her orbs as he pushed his cock into there.

The sensation of it inside of her immediately drove her mad. She gasped, feeling everything immediately go blank as he started to fuck her ass with small motions, enjoying the tightness. But, she wanted him to go faster, and with a small voice, she voiced that very need.

"Give me more," she said.

"You sure babygirl?"

"Yes. I want more," she said.

He smiled, moving his hips slowly, but then thrusting faster and faster, enjoying the actions that he was feeling. Everything was maddening, and it was then when, after a few more thrusts, he then started to hold her there as he practically jackhammered his cock into her tight asshole.

For Veronica, this was a pleasure that she never thought she would get to experience, but then, after a few more thrusts, she could feel his hands rubbing her clit, in the way that she loved it, and as she felt this, her body keened to the touch, moaning out loud at the sensations that were bestowed to her.

"Yes! Fuck yes!" she cried out.

It was only a moment later that she came hard, her entire body losing control, and everything becoming almost surreal in a sense. It was then when, after a few more thrusts, she felt him groan out loud, and he soon came inside her ass.

She shuddered at the warm feeling of his cock deep within her, but then, after a few more thrusts, he then pulled out, looking at her with a loving glance.

"You good?" he asked.

"Very good," she said. It was so much better than she anticipated, that's for sure.

"Would you do that again babygirl?" he asked.

In truth, Veronica wanted to. She wanted to feel her sugar daddy's cock deep within her, and it was then when she nodded, smiling at him.

"But of course," she replied.

"Well, I can certainly cater to that need, if that's what you want," he said to her.

She smiled at him, and she knew for a fact that she was enjoying this far more than she thought that she would. Everything about this was heavenly, that's for sure, and it was after a moment that she laid there on the bed with her sugar daddy there. He did give her money, but she was just happy serving someone that she cared about a lot.

A Rock Star's Need

Nick didn't expect his groupie Sandra to stick around after the show, but she was there, hanging out with him for a while. Nick thought Sandra was fucking gorgeous, and he loved fucking her whenever she wanted. But tonight, she seemed a bit off, and Nick felt the urge to have her.

"Something the matter?" he asked.

"Yeah. it's just...I've wanted to request something for a long time, but I didn't know how to ask," she said.

A request? What the hell could she possibly want? He looked at her, and then she blushed.

"Well, what I want is to have you fuck my ass," she said, a flush present on her face.

He looked at her, and in a sense he wondered if she read his mind or something.

"Funny, I really want this too," he said with a purr.

"I mean you don't have to if you don't want to! it's just something I've considered trying," she admitted.

He leaned in, giving her a kiss, and it was then when he smiled back.

"Trust me my dear, I definitely want this as much as you do. I mean, we can make this work," he told her.

She began to blush crimson again, but not before she laid down on the tour bus bed and blushed.

"Well, if you want to, my ass is ready," she said.

He loved the way her butt looked, and the fact that she was so ready to explore made nick hard as a rock. He reached forward, stroking Sandra's ass and giving it a small smack. She blushed once again, and then, it made him want to do more, so much more.

He pressed a digit against her entrance, testing to see if she liked it. When he heard the purr of approval, he realized that she indeed did want this, and that this was definitely something that he could get used to. It was a tight heat that practically sucked him in, and that's when he started to move his hands slightly, pressing in deep against her with soft motions.

She responded by letting out the cutest moans possible. He didn't expect her to enjoy this, but as he prepared her ass, he could feel her practically whimpering for more. When he pulled back, he spread her open, causing her to gasp.

"I'm sorry, this is just something I've wanted," she said.

"This is something I think I've wanted deep down as well," he admitted.

He touched the little pucker, watching her squirm, but then, he pressed his tongue there, rimming her with small strokes. As he did that, she let out a sudden gasp, immediately enraptured by what he was doing.

The truth was, Nick wanted to do this for a long time, and the fact that he was so enraptured by the way her ass looked in front of him, the way that the pucker was just begging for him, made him shiver with delight. He wanted this, and he knew that she did too.

With a couple more strokes, he pulled back, his cock achingly hard in his pants.

"Are you sure about this?" he asked.

"Yes. I want this. Give it to me," she told him, desperation obvious in her eyes.

He could tell that was the green light to go. After a brief moment, he pushed her legs apart, pressing his cock into her ass, and as he sank into there, he started to moan.

It felt so nice, so perfect, and whenever he pushed himself all the way in and started to move, he enjoyed every single aspect of it. He started to thrust in and out of her with small, exact motions, causing her to let out a series of cries as he began to fuck her softly, but then his need to go harder began to take over, and it was then when he started to push his cock in deeper, plunging himself all the way into her. When he finally got there, he looked at her once again, and she looked completely enraptured by the way that he was fucking her. He began to thrust in and out, taking each thrust as deep as possible until he felt like his cock couldn't take it anymore. He went in a rhythm, desperate to fuck her, and his whole body aching for more.

After a few more thrusts, Nick moved up, playing with her pussy, and he remembered that she was sensitive. That was enough to get her to cry out, moaning out loud as she came hard against him. The tightness of her ass at that point immediately made him groan in pleasure, and it was then when, after a couple more thrusts, he came hard, his body tingling as he filled her with his seed.

Everything about this felt perfect, and when he finished up, he pulled out, looking at her with expectant eyes.

"You good?" he inquired.

"Better than good," she told him.

"I'm glad. Because I want to make sure that you're taken care of as well," he said.

"You've done that and so much more. I...I love it," she admitted.

He reached in, touching her hair and looking into her eyes. She was a mere groupie, but she was someone that he could enjoy, and it made the rockstar life less insane.

"You know, I'm happy to have you, and I'm definitely happy to know that you're here with me. I think it's safe to say that you certainly do make life way more fun," he told her with a smile.

"I'm glad. I know how ti can be, the rockstar life taking a lot out of you and all," she admitted.

"Yeah, I feel that. But, I'm here and I'm happy," he said.

They stayed together for a bit, and while he knew that they couldn't be together forever due to the fact that he was a rockstar, he was definitely a happier guy.

Her New Boss

When Karen heard that her new boss was a younger guy, she immediately was on the prowl. At first, it was little touches and gestures, but then it evolved into subtle touches and little tingles that made her squirm. She loved everything about this, and she knew that he did as well.

Of course, Karen and her new boss Cody started talking, and Karen, being the hot cougar that she was, knew for a fact that she was going to certainly have a lot of fun with this. When she looked at him, she noticed his eyes always gazing at her ass. She did have a good butt, but she was surprised that he was so forthright about it.

A couple months passed, and Karen decided to test these waters. She would let his hand move towards her butt, barely touching there, and when he looked at her, instead of anger, there was something else.

Lust.

He wanted this, and she did as well. He soon moved his hands downwards, letting his hands move towards the two orbs, caressing them there. As she looked at him, he then moved over towards her hole, touching it through the confines of her thong.

'Someone seems interested,"Karen said.

She knew that she was playing a dangerous game, but it was a game that she was willing to play. He slyly smiled, and then, after a moment or so, he pulled back.

"I mean, if you want..."

She quickly pushed him over to his office, closing the door and furiously making out with him. She started to watch as he groaned, the excitement immediately hitting his pants. After getting off of him and moving towards his cock, she lightly lapped at it, and then took it halfway down her throat. She hummed, watching as he suddenly tensed up, moaning out loud and in pleasure.

"That's right, you like that don't you?" she purred.

He then pulled her head up, and then, he stopped, looking at her with a serious glance.

"It's not me I'm interested in, it's you. I want your ass," he said.

She flushed, realizing what he was saying, and soon, before she knew it, he had his hand near her pucker, teasing it with the smallest of strokes. He then moved his hand towards there, and then, after he fetched the lube that was in his drawer and pouring the contents on here, he looked at her, smiling.

"You good?" he asked her.

"Yeah. I want this," she told him with a smile on her face.

He put the first digit in there, and although the hole was tighter than he expected, she keened into the touch, moaning out loud at the sensations that this brought her. He started to finger her ass as he kissed her, adding in a second digit to the fray. She sighed, feeling everything change within her, and soon, before she knew it, he pushed a third into there. Each of these digits greeted her hungry ass, all of them sinking in, and it was then when she looked at him, and she noticed it.

He was enjoying this just as much as she was.

She couldn't believe what was happening, but here she was, horny and desperate, with three fingers in her ass, and soon, he pulled them out.

"You want to ride it cowgirl?" he asked.

"Don't mind if I do," she purred.

She moved her body so that she was right over the very tip of his cock, her ass teasing the very tip of it with tantalizing motions. After he groaned in need, she slipped her body down, watching as he threw his head back and moaned.

"What's the matter? Enjoying this?" she asked.

"Y-yes," he finally managed to reply.

She smiled at him, pressing her ass down completely, and then, he moaned once again. She started to ride him, watching with satisfaction as the man sat back, taking in the sights. She was so happy she got a chance to do this. She knew that this man was the type who wouldn't be able to resist her. She began to move her body up and down, watching as her ass began to hit the very base of his cock. She groaned, feeling everything start to get deeper over time. She watched as he started to moan as well, each and every single motion making him drool with desire. For her, she knew that it was the beginning of more fun, and then she started to pick up the pace.

Karen knew that she was doing him in. he moaned, each and every single groan that emitted from his mouth making her want to ride him harder, so that's what she did. With each one, she saw the desperation in his eyes, the need for her to continue with this, and the desire for so much more. It was the beginning of a new relationship, she knew this for sure.

She did acknowledge it was taboo, but as she continued to thrust down on his cock, he moaned out loud, and when he came, she moaned, touching herself and getting herself off as well. He watched as she pressed two fingers inside, snaking them up and touching her insides with each and every single succulent touch. She gasped, cumming hard, and he got to watch the spectacle right in front of her.

When it was all said and done, Karen pulled off of him, smiling at him with a smirk.

"You good sweetie?" she said.

"Yeah. That was just...wow," he said.

"I know, it was something. But I'm glad that you enjoyed it. Perhaps we can have some more fun too," she said.

Karen gave him a kiss, and she knew that the younger man wasn't going to say no. she clicked her heels away, smiling at her antics. Of course, her thoughts were confirmed when she got a text about ten minutes later saying the following:

I would love to do that again.

Ditching the Party

"This is lame," Lance said as he looked at Sherri.

"I have to stay here. My dad is definitely not going to be happy if I leave. This is his gala, and I'm his daughter," she said.

"Yeah and I'm just some errand boy. But don't you feel like you could do so much more? Like you could easily ditch this shitty place," he said.

Sherri sighed. She wished that she could leave. But then, Lance jumped the fence, smiling.

"You know we are going to get in trouble," she admonished.

"Come on Sherri, let's ditch this place," he said.

She looked at him, thinking he was utterly insane for doing any of this, but she followed him, and soon, they were at his house. When they got inside, she laid down on the bed, sighing.

"This is the life," she said.

"You're telling me. Better than a party, isn't it?" he asked.

She blushed, but then nodded. "You're right. It is.

"Anyways, I was thinking we do something a bit different tonight," he offered.

She tensed, looking at him with worry. "Like what.

"Like, I want to try fucking your ass," he said.

104

She blushed, but then she spoke.

"I mean, I've never done it before," she admitted.

"Yeah but, don't you think it's better to try something new rather than sit at that dumb party," he told her.

He did have a point. She nodded, sighing.

"Yeah, you're right," she admitted.

"Anyways, let's try this," he said.

She looked at him, and soon, he started to kiss her. She kissed him back, and the two of them let their tongues mingle with a pleasurable sensation for a little while, both of them enjoying the feeling of this. As they continued to make out, he pushed his hand to her plush ass, and as he did so, Sherri threw her blonde hair back, moaning in pleasure at the way he touched her. He moved his hand up, stroking her pucker as he teased her through her panties.

"You good with this?"

For Sherri, she didn't expect this to feel so...good. She expected it to be something wrong, that she would hate, but in truth, she liked the way this felt, and when she moaned, he took that as a good sign.

"Good girl," he said, playing with her once again. Sherri moaned, feeling excited about all of this. He continued to smile at her, playing with her ass as he continued to make out with her. He pressed a finger in once again, but then pulled out, grasping a bottle of lube he kept for this moment.

"I've been preparing," he admitted.

"Oh really now," Sherri said with a smirk.

Lance looked at her with a mischievous glance, but then he pushed another finger in. both of these fingers sank into her, and when she felt these, she tensed up, moaning out loud at the sensation. He pressed them in and out, letting each of them move deep within her. She then started to feel her body become even more stuffed than she thought he would make her feel. Everything was amazing, and then, as if on cue, he pulled his fingers out.

"How do you want to do it?" he asked.

Sherri paused, thinking about how she should do this. It was then when she spoke.

"I mean, missionary works. it's my first time," she said.

Lance nodded, spreading her apart and lining his cock up against her hole.

"Tell me if it hurts," he said.

She nodded, and soon he pushed the tip in, watching as she threw her head back, crying out loud at the sensation of being spread apart. He then moved in deeper, letting his cock sink into her, and at first, she thought about telling him no, she couldn't do this. But, she didn't want to disappoint him, and then, as soon as she thought that, the pain went away.

"What the heck?" she said.

"What's wrong?"

"It feels...good," she admitted.

"Well good, that's how I want it to feel," he teased.

He started to move his hips against her, thrusting his cock as deep as he could. For Sherri, at first it was a bit painful, but then, it hit a spot that made her tense up, and when it did, she cried out in pleasure at the sensation that she felt.

"Fuck!" she cried out.

She definitely was enjoying this. He smiled, continuously fucking her tight ass with his cock. She held onto him for dear life, and as he continued to fuck her relentlessly, she soon felt as if everything was driving her to the point of madness.

She was so close already. She knew that it was something that she couldn't hold back, and when he reached forward, massaging her clit as he fucked her, she knew that this was the beginning of it. When he pushed against it, she screamed out loud, letting her hips move up and her pussy throb. She came, and the tightness was too much for Lance. He tried very hard to keep himself together, trying to make sure that he didn't cum too fast, but it was too late. He shivered, cumming hard inside of her, causing her to let out a sudden gasp in pleasure at the sensation of this.

"Holy fuck," she said.

"You good?" he inquired.

"Better than good," she told him.

He reached forward, pulling her close and kissing her. She kissed him back, and soon he pulled away, smiling at her.

"Better than sticking around at some boring party, don't you think," he teased.

Sherri nodded, lightly elbowing him.

"Okay fine, maybe you were right and it was better than a party," she teased.

"I know I'm right, because I see it on your face," he replied back.

She smiled, feeling a strange feeling wash over her.e she wanted to do this again, wanted to feel him fuck her ass again, and she knew that it was better than a party, that's for fucking sure.

Work Breaks Made Fun

It was another boring work day, but at least Izzy and Andrew got to work together. As the cafe's newest and hottest couple, people would congratulate them, but of course Izzy and Andrew hadn't had much time together.

Which was why, during their break in the break room Andrew locked the door, pushing Izzy against the wall and making out with her with a fervency that even she was supersized about. She kissed him back, feeling the need grow within her as time started to pass on by. Soon, Andrew had her up against the wall, his hands right near her round ass, touching the cheeks.

"You look so good," he said to her.

"Thank you," she moaned, feeling his hands massage the area. It felt so nice, so perfect, but then, he started to slide her pants off. She knew what was coming.

Andrew had recently tried anal with Izzy, and to say that it woke up some monster within him was an understhatement. He loved it, and for some reason, he grew almost addicted to it, and as he started to tease the puckered flesh, she began to moan, feeling excited about everything that was happening. She started to move towards the touch, feeling everything begin to change within her. It was heavenly, and then, as if on cue, he pushed his finger into her.

She didn't know he even lubed it up but when it was inside, she let out a moan that was a bit of a surprise, but also a relaxed one. He began to push his fingers in and out of her, starting with the smallest of touches and then moving towards the inner thigh. When he pushed his fingers in, she tensed up, gasping I surprise at the sensation of being filled up. He then started to press his fingers in and out of her, watching as she moaned, feeling everything as he continued to do this. Each and every single touch was enough to drive her mad, and then, after a few more thrusts, he added in a second finger.

Izzy learned that she really liked anal as well. At first, she thought that it was wrong, but then she r3slized that it gave her intense pleasure, and she soon pushed her butt against the two fingers inside of her, causing him to groan as the ring of muscle sucked his fingers in. watching as she got off to this was something that she enjoyed, and then, she noticed that he was already hard as a rock. When she pulled back, she smiled at him, a coy little grin that said it all.

"You want to stick it in," she said.

Andrew knew that the only had about fifteen more minutes. Nobody figured out that this was what they did on their breaks, but he soon pushed his hands to the side, spreading her cheeks and then, with awkward hands, he covered his fingers in lube and then rubbed his cock, looking at the two wonderful moons that were there.

"Fuck," he said to himself.

He watched as she gasped at the feeling of his hands as he began to spread her cheeks apart, and then the feeling of his lubed up cock as he started to penetrate her hard.

She gasped, tensing up at the sensations that were happening within her. She loved this, and she knew that with him, this was the type of feeling that she wanted to have. He began to fuck her with a fervency that she loved, and he soon started to press his cock as deep as he could into her. She immediately moaned, tensing up and pushing her body against his own. The sensation of his cock inside of her tight ass made her want more, and it was then that, after a few more thrusts, she knew that they needed to finish up soon.

It was obvious that they only had a limited amount of time, and it was then when he started to thrust into her hard, and she met his own. He pressed his fingers towards her clit, rubbing it so that she could get off, and then, after inserting a finger into her pussy with everything else, they both stopped, the sudden feeling of cumming immediately overwhelming their senses.

The first to cum was Andrew, and he filled her ass up with his seed. He groaned at the sensation of the feeling that he shared, and as he looked at her, he noticed that she was enjoying this just as much. After a few more moments, she let out a sudden gasp, feeling everything become blank as she rode his cock, cumming hard as a result of his actions.

She watched as he pulled away, a little bit of cum moving out of her hole. She reached over, grabbing a couple of paper towels to clean up the excess. Quickly, they both got their clothes on, looking at one another with lustful glances.

"God your ass is so much fun to get into," he said.

"Look who's talking, your cock feels amazing in there," she said with a flush on her face.

He looked at her, smiling warmly, and soon, both of them started to kiss one another hard. The sensation of this was almost too much, and they knew that if they continued in this line, they'd end up fucking once again. But then, he pulled away, smiling.

"Let's do this later," he said.

"You think tonight after our shift?" she asked with a purr.

Andrew smiled, knowing this. "Yeah, I'm cool with that," he told her.

She gave him one last kiss before she pulled away, winking.

"Good. We should probably get back to work though. Don't want anyone to think we're doing some naughty now, would we?" she teased.

Andrew blushed, but he followed her, and soon, they were back to the tedium of life, their jobs, but they still had one another.

What to Do Instead of Hitting the Books

The last thing Sally and Brendan wanted to do was study. Fuck finals, and fuck the element of studying. Plus, it didn't help that Brendan was very attractive, and Sally was having trouble focusing.

"You okay there Sally?" he inquired.

"Oh! Yeah I'm okay," she said.

"You sure? You look a bit distracted, you know," he said.

"No it's just...I have something on my mind," she said.

"Like what?"

Sally blushed, wondering what her friend might say. She then took a deep breath, looking at him with a red face.

"Have you ever...thought about anal?" she asked.

"What brought that up?" he asked with a laugh.

"Don't make fun of me, but I was watching some porn the other night, and I saw it and like...I wanted to try it," she told Brendan with a blush.

Brendan looked at Sally with surprise.

"Are you sure? It tends to hurt."

"I'm sure. I mean, it's something I've been curious about, you know," she admitted with a flush on her face. As Brendan heard this, he blushed as well, surprised by how forthright she was with this.

"Well, I guess we can try it," he told her.

"Okay. I want to," she said.

He then looked at her, tossing the textbook to the side and kissing her.

"Fuck studying. Not worth it," he said.

She then kissed him back, moaning in surprise and shock at the sensations that he gave to her. He soon started to kiss her harder and harder, each and every single touch driving her mad. He then pushed her down, pulling her skirt up and letting his tongue lick the edge of her pussy. Brendan knew that he wanted to get her off first before he tried anything like this.

Sure enough, it did them both good. Sally immediately whimpered, crying out loud at the sensations that were bestowed to her. She knew that he was enjoying this as much as she was, and soon, they both were making sounds of satisfaction, and of desire.

For Sally, she loved being eaten out, but she was curious about butt stuff. She did buy lube, and she did get a toy at one point, and she knew for a fact that this was the sensation that she wanted to feel. She soon looked at him, and soon he grabbed the contents pressing a singular finger into her.

"You good?" he asked.

The sensation of her ass being filled with something like this was...strange that's for sure. She didn't expect it to feel so foreign, so different from what she was used to, but she soon moaned, bucking her hips in happiness and pleasure as he started to push the digit in deeper and deeper. The sensation was almost too much for her, and as he pushed in deep, she tensed up.

He continued slowly, feeling her relax to his touch, but then he started to insert a second, and she felt filled up once again. She began to moan as he started to push his fingers in and out of her, loving the feeling of her tight ass against his fingers. He continued with the third digit, waiting until she was ready for the real thing, and then, when he pulled back he patted the bed.

"I'm going to sit down. I want you to ride me," he said.

She blushed. Sally had a feeling that the reason for this was because she didn't want him to hurt her, and he was hesitant about taking control the first time. Sure enough, she soon pushed herself against the tip, feeling it fill her up, and then, Sally wondered if she made the right decision.

It was tight. Almost too tight, and when she felt him get all the way in, she shuddered. She didn't know if this was it, but then, when he was finally inside, it soon got easier. She then relaxed, liking the tightness, and when she started to move, she noticed it hit a part of her body that she was definitely not used to.

She started to cry out loud, feeling the pleasure sink through her body. After a couple more thrusts, she noticed that Brendan was sitting there, ogling her body.

"You're beautiful," he told her.

"Thank you," she replied, feeling everything become almost magical as she continued to ride his cock. The sensations were overwhelming, that's for sure, but she loved the feeling of this, and then after a few more thrusts, she soon tensed up, crying out loud in pleasure.

She came hard, feeling her entire body lose control at the sensations that were there. He soon pushed himself all the way down, and when he groaned, he felt his cock empty out, filling her up completely with his seed. She shuddered, for it was a different sensation than how it felt when he came inside of her pussy, but she wasn't complaining, that's for sure.

When he finished, she pulled back, blushing red.

"That was just...wow," she said.

"Good for you?"

"Yeah. Amazing, really," she admitted.

"Well, I'm glad I could help then," he said to her.

The two of them looked at one another, kissing once again. Sure enough, their study session took a very different turn, but neither of them were complaining. Rather, they were both happy and satisfied with the feelings that they shared.

"I wouldn't mind doing that kind of studying again," Brendan said.

"Same here. But next time, we should make sure that we have our work finished before we consider doing that," she admitted.

"I think that's a smart move," he admitted to her.

She laughed, planting a kiss on his lips.

"You know, I never thought that it would feel this good. I'm happy," she admitted.

"I'm happy as well," he told her.

Both of them smiled, their eyes glistening with happiness, the desire growing within them. For Sally she felt that this was the beginning of something more, but she didn't want to push it. But it was better than studying, that's for sure.

Paying Her Debt

Jackie felt the familiar tightness in her ass as Dan began to press the toy into her, turning it on.

"You have to keep it in my dear, or else that's another 500 added to your debt. But, if you manage to make me cum with your ass I'lll take away 2000," he said to her.

She blushed, and as she felt him push the toy in deeper, turning on the vibrations, she began to shudder, the excitement filling her body as he began to penetrate her deeper. She began to tense up, feeling everything change, and as she began to feel him push the toy right up against that spot that drove her crazy, she felt her entire body start to sweat.

"Fuck," she muttered, feeling everything go blank.

"You handle it?" he asked, his voice almost mocking.

"I can," she spat back with confidence. Course, even she didn't know for sure what might happen. He clicked it up higher, and she soon cried out.

The one thing about Jackie was that she came from anal play, and when she bit her lip getting close, she realized over time that she may not be able to hold her ground. She then tensed up, gasping out loud as she felt her entire body shake at the sensation of her orgasm.

Dan loved seeing her come undone whenever she came too hard. She was a total mess right now, moaning and gasping in pleasure at the sensations that were happening, and he smiled, knowing that he was the one to create those. After he turned off the toy, he pulled it out, looking at her with a smile.

"You did so well my dear. I think it's safe to say that you're ready for me. And, you still were able to reduce your debt by 500," he said.

"Thank you sir,"Jackie said.

Jackie had this debt for as long as she could remember, but she was just now taking her life back. Dan was a rich businessman who found her on the street, offering her a chance to take care of it. What she didn't know, was that she was going to use her body for this.

But, his large, thick cock was right there, a familiar sight to her, and as she looked at him, she realized that he looked bigger than usual.

"Did you get thicker?" she asked.

"I've been trying these enhancement pills. I didn't think so, but that's really up to you," he said.

She shivered, realizing the truth of all of this. She was at the mercy of his actions. She watched as he stroked himself completely, looking at her body.

"God you're so pretty," he said.

"Thank you," Jackie replied.

He positioned himself so that his cock was right near her entrance, and then with a groan, he pushed himself into her.

She tensed up, feeling his thick cock completely breach her walls. She screamed out loud, shocked by the sudden feeling of this, and as he started to push himself deep inside, she began to shiver, feeling as if she was about to get broken by this man.

Would he break her? Would he actually completely destroy her? She didn't even know, but when he thrusted his fat cock into her completely, she let out a sudden scream, her entire body losing control at the feelings she was feeling.

"Fuck," she cried out loud. She was whimpering by this point, and that's when she felt Dan give her a hard smack on the backside.

"Come on, take it," he said to her.

He started to press himself deeper and deeper, fucking her faster than she was used to. She had to endure this. She had to make him cum.

She knew that if she did that, she would at least get closer to her debt being paid, which was something that she didn't mind.

She started to feel him push himself into her at a faster pace, and she felt as if she was being split in half. But, when he managed to make it so that he was hitting the bundle of nerves there, she screamed out loud, shuddering in pleasure at the sensation that she was feeling.

"Holy fuck," she said, feeling as if everything was driving her insane.

He continued his onslaught against her body, watching as she shivered, loving every single moment of this, and then, as soon as she felt him press all the way in, he tensed up, and she lightly gasped as he touched her clit with the smallest touch.

He came hard into her, and the sensation of cumming inside of her sent something through her body, a shiver of sorts, and she soon lost her mind.

"Holy shit," she said to him.

She then started to gasp, feeling as if everything was on fire. She then started to tense up, feeling her body soon reach the brink of orgasm. As quick as it happened, she then relaxed, riding out her orgasm.

"Holy crap," she finally managed to say after it was all said and done.

"You like it, kitten?" he asked.

"Yeah. That was something all right," she admitted.

"Well, you managed to get another two grand off your debt. You still have a long ways to go, but with that ass of yours, I'm sure you'll manage to get this paid off in no time.

He left Jackie on the floor there, a shivering mess with cum trailing down her leg. She then realized that her ass did have the power to get her out of this mess, and although she was doing this to pay off her debt, she wasn't going to complain, because it also felt amazing as well, and she also felt that it was something she did enjoy, even if she did have ulterior motives for doing everything that she did with this man at the moment.